Linnea A. Due

HIGH

AND

OUT-

SIDE

spinsters|*aunt lute*
SAN FRANCISCO

First Spinsters/Aunt Lute Edition 1988
10-9-8-7-6-5-4-3-2-1

Spinsters/Aunt Lute Book Company
P.O. Box 410687
San Francisco, CA 94141

Cover Design: Pam Wilson Design Studio
Cover Photos: Avery McGinn
Text Design: Trish Parcell

Production: Martha Davis   Jeanette Hsu
               Debra DeBondt   Cindy Lamb

Spinsters/Aunt Lute is an educational project
of the Capp Street Foundation

Printed in the U.S.A.

Library of Congress Cataloging-in-Publication Data
Due, Linnea A.
  High and outside.
Originally published: New York: Harper & Row, 1980
  I. Title.
PS3554.U314H5 1988   813'.54   88-23825
ISBN 0-933216-60-2
ISBN 0-933216-58-0 (pbk.)

For my parents

HIGH
AND
OUT-
SIDE

Chapter I

When I saw the starters for Washington High, I was glad I stopped with dinner wine last night and didn't graduate on to my usual couple of beers. Washington must have recruited some semi-pros or something. Those girls looked about as much like sixteen- or seventeen-year-olds as I look like Grandma Moses.

Scotty was slumped over on the bench, probably wishing she had one of those smelly black cigarettes she smokes. "Hey," I said. "How 'bout checking a couple of drivers' licenses?"

Scotty couldn't dredge up enough energy to smile. "It's all by good faith in high school softball," she said. "I don't suppose their coach would try anything funny, though they do look awfully old. I don't know," she finished hopelessly, "just do the best you can."

For the coach of the champion interschool team, she sure sounded depressed. I shrugged. "We'll do O.K.," I said. "I'm going to warm up." I spun off down the third-base line and started firing fastballs to Sarah, my catcher. But I couldn't concentrate too well, wondering what was bothering Scotty. It was probably the allocation. The school district didn't have a lot of money, and eliminating one of the boys' sports would never enter the minds of our hale and hearty city fathers. Our softball team, the only women's activity besides a couple of divers on the swim team, would be the sport to get cut. Scotty would have to go back to being a plain old gym teacher in a reasonably good city high school.

When I finally got up on the mound, the breeze worried at my hair, and I shot my hand up angrily, pushing my hair behind my ears. All right, I thought, now I'm psyched, set, and ready or not— I flung a scorcher straight across the plate. The batter swung, and the ball skidded down third base, hot as a bullet from a .45. Ginny scooped it up and tossed it to Martha at first. She juggled it around before she managed to control it. "One out!" I yelled. "Go, go!" The chatter swelled behind me. When I noticed Martha looking sheepish, I grinned at her. "It's cool," I shouted. "You got her out, didn't you?"

The next batter looked six feet tall, and I wasted two balls below her knees before I got the range. Then I overcompensated and floated a beauty right in, and she smacked it out to left field. Our fielders aren't the greatest. She got a standing double before our shortstop had the ball in her glove.

"Idiot!" I mumbled to myself, and in a rage struck out the next batter one-two-three. But then their hot number came up, their sweep hitter. She sliced a beauty over toward center field, and Washington High had one run. Thank God I managed to strike out number five. We trotted into our dugout and I pulled on my jacket. "Good pitching, Niki," everybody mumbled, but I could see they were worried. Fear hovered just outside the circle of stoney faces, and I wished I could think of something to say to calm everybody down. I couldn't help with my bat. In five years of softball I'd never hit out of the infield.

2

By the fourth inning, we were down four to nothing. I knew we'd break out of our doldrums if we could get a run. Scotty hadn't said anything yet, but it turned out she was thinking the same thing. "All right, you seniors," she snapped. The three seniors bobbed their heads. "This is the last year you'll be playing for Lincoln. You want to be on a losing team? I want some hits. I want some people on bases. I want a run up on that scoreboard. Out of the three of you, we oughta be able to get one little run, right? Concentrate on that."

It settled everything down. True, it put the pressure on the seniors, but they could take it. We were a mostly junior team, including myself, but the seniors were our best hitters and they knew it. Sally came up at the top of the order and hit a single. Then Martha smacked a line drive right down the third-base line, and Sally got to third. Ginny struck out, and she came back shaking her head. "Their pitcher is fast," she said.

"Move back from the plate. Stand on their catcher," Scotty counseled. She looked grim. But Teri, our shortstop, was up, and she was our top batter. She hit a homer. We yelled, "Come on, come on! Home! Home!" The scoreboard looked a whole lot better with a three on it.

When I got home, my father was already ensconced in his favorite living-room chair, swirling around the liquor in the bottom of his old fashioned glass. "Hey, Carl! How come you're back so early?" I'd started calling my parents by their first names a few years ago for a lark. When my father seemed to like it, I kept it up. By now I missed the old Mom and Dad routine, but I never would have admitted it.

He brightened when he saw me. Carl was my biggest fan. "Did you win?"

I nodded. "Pulled out of a slump in the fourth, and then went on to win by one run in the seventh. Six to five. It was a tough game."

"Washington," he mused. "They're pretty good. How's the rest of school?"

It was a joke between us—sports and the rest of school. "Same old thing," I answered. I always did well in my classes, so for pure excitement value, Carl concentrated on my athletics. Of course, if I ever came home with a C on my report card, my parents would wake up in a hurry.

I was looking at his drink. "Could I have one of those? Or actually I'd rather have a gin and tonic."

"Hmmm? Oh, O.K." He went into the kitchen and I tagged along after him. While he was making my drink, he told me to save room for the wine he'd brought up from the cellar this morning. "It's a '74 cabernet," he said. "Absolutely great. I had Johnny save me a bottle from a private shipment." Johnny worked at the liquor store. He always got a big tip at Christmas.

"Why *are* you home so early?" I asked when we'd settled back down in the living room. Wednesday and Friday were days my father actually appeared at his clients' offices. He was a consultant to a motley collection of organizations and individuals who needed his help to untangle the bureaucratic mess that's part and parcel of getting a grant. Carl described himself at parties as a modern-day prospector, and I suppose that's what he really was.

He shrugged. "Got finished sooner than I thought. The Simms Foundation came through for Dr. Buehler."

"That's great!" My father couldn't stand half the people he advised. He said his clients came up with crazy projects like "The Relationship of Color Blindness to the Effectiveness of Mass Transit Advertising Placards" so they wouldn't have to work for another year or two. He liked Dr. Buehler, though, and it was a coup to get the tight-fisted Simms Foundation to unleash some of its money. "Did you tell Joyce? Where is she, anyway?"

4

"No, I haven't told her yet. You know where she is." He gestured vaguely in the direction of the downstairs study.

"Right," I said, tapping my head with my index finger. Trust me to forget the current brouhaha at our house, namely tax time in three weeks. Joyce was bookkeeper and accountant for my father's consulting business, and she managed to create a big scene about it from March on. I could never understand how the taxes could be so messed up every year when she kept such careful track of everything.

Her voice floated up the stairway. "Has anyone checked the stew?"

"That's what was burning!" I said loudly to my father.

My mother came charging up the stairs as if there were two horses ahead of her in the stretch at the Kentucky Derby.

"A joke," Carl said. "Our daughter inherited your sense of humor."

My mother showed no propensity to humor at the moment. Bad move, I thought. "Look, Niki," she began. Then she thought of something. "Carl, do you know how much— What time is it anyway?"

"Five-thirty," I answered.

"I'll get back to it later," she decided. "Somebody make me a scotch and water." She sank onto the sofa, apparently exhausted by her struggles with the I.R.S.

"I'll do it," I offered. "I'll even stir the stew."

"All right," my mother said. She started talking about the taxes with Carl.

I went into the kitchen and mixed Joyce's drink. My father had taught me how to make all the usual cocktails when I was sixteen, around the same time he was lecturing me about social drinking. By then I'd already been drinking wine for two years, but I got the feeling Carl didn't consider wine alcohol. It was simply part of a good dinner. Cocktails came along the summer after my sophomore year, when my boyfriend Chuck

5

announced he was pledging a fraternity in the fall. I knew my father had visions of mass orgies fed by potato chips and countless kegs of beer. "There's no mystique about drinking, Niki," he told me. "Getting drunk and falling on your face is about as romantic as falling on your face sober. The only difference is it doesn't hurt as much if you're drunk."

One reason I enjoyed making the cocktails was it gave me an opportunity to freshen my own drink, plus gulp a couple of jiggers of gin on the side. I stirred the stew and sliced up some bread. When I carried in my mother's drink, she was describing the ins and outs of recent tax law changes. I swear Joyce should have been an attorney. She could spend half an hour detailing the terrible effects one less allowable deduction would have on the family bank account for at least the next twenty years. My father managed to look interested through another round of drinks, but when Joyce brought big bowls of stew to the table, he dropped all pretense and dove into his food.

I had survived the tax lecture by thinking about how I'd write up the game for the school paper. I was the editorial page editor and the reporter for our softball games. It was kind of hard to write the stories, because I couldn't by-line them. That meant they had to be pretty straight copy—no "spectacular catches" or the kind of personal anecdotes that made sports stories interesting. I felt funny if I had to mention myself. Usually I just added a line at the bottom, something like "Niki Etchen pitched her second shut-out of the season." I didn't have to worry about that this time. After all, I'd given up five runs.

Carl was pouring more wine, and it occurred to me I should make an effort to enter in the dinner conversation. My brain must have been taking a siesta, or it might have been those extra jiggers of gin. I asked my mother if she planned to drop by Robertson's any day soon—I needed some new softball socks.

She threw down her fork and stared at me, looking for all the world as if I had suggested she might spend her time profitably by digging a hole ninety feet deep in the backyard. "Are you joking? How can you possibly imagine I have time to run ridiculous errands for you when I am swamped with tax forms and billing? Honestly, Niki, you are the most thoughtless . . ."

I sighed as she rambled on. I was at the age—seventeen—when parents were probably best unseen and unheard. We all floated around like separate tankers off on long journeys, only getting together at cocktail hour and dinner to refuel. Here I was, blithely tossing matches near the oil lines. Obviously my father felt the same way, because he kicked me under the table. I grinned, trying to placate her. "Joyce, I'm sorry. I must have lost my head for a second there."

She assumed I was being sarcastic and narrowed her eyes at me. I changed the subject by asking my father about the wine. He took his cue and bounded up to show me the label, beginning a lengthy discussion about the brilliance of '74 wines. His point would be proved, he insisted, if we compared this wine with a '75 from the same winery. I had missed whatever point he was trying to make, but I was perfectly willing to go along with the wine tasting. The story on the game was the only homework I absolutely *had* to do, and that would only take a few minutes. I never got much done on Wednesdays, because I didn't get home until around cocktail hour. What was more important, I thought nobly as Carl went down to the wine cellar, the school newspaper or family harmony?

When I woke up the next morning, I was sick, sick physically and ill with a feeling that something horrible had happened the night before. I waited, lying there, willing my head to get on track and tell me what I'd done. I looked at the typewriter, and there was a sheet of paper in it. The game story, I soothed myself, but I knew it wasn't. Maybe I'd sat down last night to write up the game, but that wasn't what I'd ended up typing. I couldn't stand to look. I could barely walk. I stumbled to the kitchen and gulped down nearly a quart of orange juice. My father came in looking haggard. "Did you see this?" he asked, waving the morning *Chronicle* in my face. The Giants traded Brewster for two minor league outfielders! They must have decided we don't need an infield this year...." I made a few conciliatory noises and fled back to my room, circling around the typewriter, afraid to read what I'd written last night. God, why couldn't I pass out quietly the way normal people do? I finally ripped the sheet out of the machine and spread it on the desk. It was a mass of misspellings and misspacings, but I was used to that. I read:

How cum I cant b honeskt? I'm a person, ust like any other person,mor so in fat, and I wnat to be rocognized. You cqn sit around and t ype, nothinv matters for the nex twenty-five years, and it's true nothingm matters, expet who cares? Does the majority of the Americn public care that noghtin matters. NO! All they care about is what? Do I care about wht they care about? No! None of this make any sensewhatsoever, wgish is sad, because it made w a whole lotta sens when I wrote it. Damn. Damn. I'm so fucking lonely. Somenofy help me. I feeling like killing myself.

I tried to keep my mind a blank as I tore the paper up in lengthwise, then crosswise strips, and crumpled all the pieces and threw them down the toilet, never mind the plumbing. I scrubbed the toothbrush across my teeth, over my gums, on my tongue, trying to get rid of the stale beer taste. I couldn't remember switching to beer, but I had at some point. There was no mistaking that hungover beer breath. I suddenly got dizzy and sat on the side of the bathtub. Jesus, what was the matter with me? Why was I such a coward? "Somebody help me." *Jesus!* It was so hard to be strong, especially when all you wanted was to sleep off a hangover. One thing, killing myself, that sounded good. Anything would be better than this.

I went into the kitchen, fixed myself some eggs and toast, drank another enormous glass of juice, and chatted about baseball with my father. Neither of us mentioned my being drunk, though my parents wouldn't necessarily have noticed. After the '75 wine, they had gone on to after-dinner drinks, so they were probably feeling pretty happy themselves. I had the option of the bottle of gin hidden in the closet of my bedroom, or the beer in the bar refrigerator in the TV room, both out of sight of my parents. But even if they had seen me cruising around plastered, I wasn't sure they'd say anything. I discovered early on, around fifteen, that my occasional lapses of drunkenness fell into the same category as my mother's and father's instances of overindulgence—unfit subjects for family discussion. This unwritten rule applied to their friends too, which I'd figured out after years of cocktail parties and entertaining. All I'd receive for my effort to describe Milly Haverstraw nearly tumbling down the front steps were two frosty looks from my parents. By the time I was ten, I'd learned to keep my mouth shut. When I started drinking myself, I was glad I wasn't singled out as the family exception to the silence rule, because I couldn't bear to think up excuses or hunt for apologies with my head pounding the way it was now.

I think my parents felt getting drunk was in poor taste, and therefore better ignored, as one might avoid looking at the neighbor's yard so as not to notice the plastic pink flamingos on the lawn. Getting drunk was something people other than social drinkers like us did. My father might suggest that fraternity boys drank to get drunk, or perhaps a group of hunters off on a long weekend. But if one stuck to the normal routine of cocktails, wine with dinner, and then some liqueur or beer to settle the stomach, getting drunk could only be considered an unfortunate accident, a lightning bolt that hopefully would not strike twice.

My car started right off, and I zipped the two miles to school. I bought a Coke at the stand, grabbed a pack of antacid pills, and crumpled into my desk just as the bell rang. Thank God I had English first period. I got perpetual A's in English, no trying at all, so I could sleep through my hangovers. Which is what I did, laying my head on my arms, waking up every fifteen minutes to gulp some Coke and pop a stomach pill in my mouth. I tried to forget the paper. Could anyone read it? How? It was flushed down the toilet. Suppose the toilet spewed it back up? Maybe it was written across my face? I fought down the panic and looked at the clock. Ten more minutes. Nine more minutes. I wondered if I was going crazy, and then I fell asleep again until the bell rang.

Second period was a little better, and by lunchtime I was feeling more human. I was ravenous, and ate two hot dogs instead of my usual one, then scarfed down an orange bar too. Along with milk, three little half-pint cartons full. There! The horror of last night's insane note was going away, but it was the sort of going away that hits you full force less and less often. I kept having to bite my lip each time the panic started, hoping no one could tell. I distracted myself by spending the last ten minutes of lunch hurriedly scribbling up my report of yesterday's game. Mitch, my journalism teacher, would be irritated it was handwritten, but there was nothing I could do about it now.

When I got to the newspaper office, a big hulking sophomore thrust a headline in my hand. "This O.K.?" he said gruffly.

I looked at the press-type headline, with the letters all screwed up, tilted here and there, and suddenly blew up.

"What do you mean, is this all right? Don't you know we have to pay for this stuff? Three-fifty a sheet! Look at the spacing between this e and this r. Besides, who wrote this? 'Tigers Tankless'! That's hilarious."

When I'd finished screaming and looked up at him, I thought he was going to explode, but instead he shuffled his feet, and said, "Yeah, well, I'll try it again."

I felt like a king-sized dope. "Look, Gerry, I'm sorry. The letters in a word are almost touching, maybe a sixteenth of an inch apart. And use that black line under the letters. Put it over the blue line on your graph paper. That way the letters won't tilt. It's no big deal, but it does make the paper look better."

"It's only the school paper," he said plaintively before he walked away. I closed my eyes and wished I was back home in bed asleep, not here having to hassle with everyone. I stared out of the window at the Golden Gate Bridge across the bay, hoping I'd calm down. My mind snapped back to when I was twelve, down in Carmel, gathering crabs and sea urchins and anemones for a tide-pool aquarium. I saw myself there, in the sea breeze, scrambling over cliffs, sneakers gripping to rocks, grabbing at crabs carefully so I wouldn't hurt them. The breakers plunged into crevices and sucked out again slowly, and I'd wait with a rock hammer till the water was only a foot deep, and then slip in and pound at an anemone-covered rock until I had to jump back out. I remembered how I felt that day, free and salt-whipped, a healthy young animal in charge of my own future. I'd wanted more than anything to be a marine biologist, to explore islands in the Pacific, to chart ocean currents and study fish migrations, to be outdoors or hunched over a microscope in a laboratory. It had all seemed possible when I was twelve. I'd had no doubt that was what was in store for me. I could do anything.

I looked at the wall and almost started crying. How come everything got so complicated all of a sudden? I felt as if I was carrying stones on top of my shoulders, and they prevented me from even thinking straight. Why couldn't I be a marine biologist? But I had the feeling that was lost, all that ambition, though I didn't know why. I wished I could be that unafraid kid again, standing on the cliff, looking out at the ocean as if she owned it. Maybe that was it. Maybe I'd become a coward. The paper with "Somebody help me" flashed into my head again, and my stomach turned over. There was something the matter with me. It was crazy to feel this deep melancholy for your childhood when you were only seventeen. I should drive to Carmel and look at the sea. I might be all right then.

That idea kept me going until the wrap-up meeting of yesterday's game was over, and when I got home, I snarled at Joyce and retired to my room. I whipped through my homework, my father came in from a consultation, and it was cocktail hour. Or cocktail two hours was more like it, complete with the daily tax report and my father's grousing about tight money. My mother got on him about that, because we weren't supposed to discuss unpleasant things during cocktails. The whole point of cocktail hour, my mother maintained, was that it was a time to relax and be together as a family. My father defended himself by saying anything Joyce wanted to talk about, such as taxes, was pleasant, and whatever he wanted to talk about was nasty and forbidden. This argument had been going on as long as I could remember.

I didn't really feel like drinking, so I bagged my gin and tonics and had a Coke instead. My father had resurrected another wine from oblivion at the liquor store, so all of us had to sample it with dinner. Poor Carl. If he only knew I wasn't too thrilled with wine. He was so happy filling up our glasses, beaming at us as he asked, "Well? What do you think?" I always made the appropriate comments about smoothness or bite, bouquet and aftertaste. He would listen carefully, then smile at Joyce. "She's really something, isn't she?" Joyce would mutter about giving me a swelled head, and Carl would scoff. "Nonsense, Niki's far too sensible for that." It was one of my deepest suspicions that my mother didn't appreciate wine either.

Martha called me at nine. "What are you doing?"

"Drinking a beer," I answered. Dinner had gotten me in the mood for beer.

"Yeah, you," Martha sighed. Martha's parents didn't drink, which I never really believed, because I didn't know any adults who didn't drink. I figured they didn't want Martha to know, and they kept bottles hidden in the garage or something. Weird. "You coming to the party Saturday?"

I sucked at my beer. "I don't know," I said. "I've been thinking about going down to Carmel."

"Oh, yeah? That's nice. Who with?"

"Myself," I answered. But then I got scared. "You wanta come?" I asked weakly.

"Me? Are you crazy? I'm really up for this party. I got Greg to buy me a fifth of scotch when he was home on vacation, and I've had it hidden in my room all month. It's going to be a real blowout. Why don't you go to Carmel next weekend instead?"

I thought. It was true, big crazo booze parties didn't come along every day, and I could go to Carmel any time. Besides, I hadn't been to a party since Chuck and I broke up, and that was New Year's Eve—three months ago. Maybe that's why I felt so weak lately. I was getting too isolated, too crammed into my own head. All you need is some fun, I told myself. "Sure," I said to Martha, who was beginning to make impatient noises. "I'll pick you up around nine."

After I'd hung up the phone, I wandered into the TV room, thinking about Chuck. I hadn't seen him since that night I refused to go to his dumb fraternity party. . . . Here I'd gotten us in a real bar for New Year's Eve, and he wanted to leave the first bar either of us had ever been in to go to his frat house! I started getting irritated, and I stopped myself. I'd picked apart every facet of the scene at the bar a thousand times already. I always came to the same conclusion: he had his reasons for wanting to leave, and I had mine for wanting to stay. The way we broke up didn't matter. We'd been heading in that direction for a while, and neither of us had been able to turn things around. The only thing that mattered now was his absence caused me a lot of pain.

Martha had introduced us the summer before I started high school, when I was fifteen. Chuck was two years older. It wasn't exactly love at first sight. We hung out together, went to movies, discussed books, had arguments about politics and religion. Then he went away for a month over Christmas with his father, which turned out to be the first of several separations before his parents got divorced. Chuck and I missed each other a lot. Our first letters mentioned being lonely. Then we talked about how we longed for each other. Finally we got down to loving each other. The day he was supposed to turn up at my house, we were both nervous. Love is a lot easier to express by letter, especially when it takes you by surprise.

Actually, our meeting was easy. I heard him knock, I opened the door, and he glowed like a giant firefly when I told him how happy I was to see him. He kept muttering he was twice as happy to see me. We ended up bickering, then laughing, and finally we went out and walked around in the park in a daze for a few hours. From then on, we were together almost every minute for more than a year.

Martha was pretty excited about the whole thing. She kept running around telling everybody she had introduced us, and

14

she told me how lucky I was. "He's the only decent guy in our school. Intelligent, good-looking, nice—you've got it made."

Oh, I had it made, all right, until it started to go downhill. I noticed Chuck began to criticize me about a lot of dumb things, like my playing sports in college. "You won't want to be on any teams," he said one day. "Only female jocks go on with athletics on the college level. It's O.K. now, of course, when you're still in high school." This said from his lofty position as a two-month-old college freshman.

"I like sports," I insisted. "I like the competition, I like the feeling of being skilled at something. I'm good. I'm not giving that up for fear some lame-ass is going to call me a female jock."

At the time, these arguments infuriated me. Now it was easier to look back and see he didn't really care about whether I played sports in college, or what editorials I wrote, or any of the other things he chose to criticize. He was frustrated. We were discovering we didn't like to do the same things. Even though Chuck was quiet, he enjoyed being around a lot of people, especially after his parents broke up. I was more of a lone wolf. I preferred to read a book or take a walk. Big groups of people scared me unless I was loaded, and Chuck complained I ignored him when I was drunk. Impasse. Chuck frustrated and lonely in one corner, me shy and lonely in the other. I still couldn't understand why we hadn't been able to change things so it would work.

Forget it, I thundered inside. What's the point of all these post-mortems? It's finished. I forced myself to concentrate on the party Saturday night. Parties were fun when you drank. That's why people went to parties. And fun was what I needed. Chuck— Stop it! I jumped up and punched on the TV. What you need more than fun, I thought, is complete mindlessness. I should put in an application for a frontal lobotomy.

Chapter II

When I pulled up at the traffic light, I reached behind me and patted the paper bag with the beer in it. Still there. I'd bought tall cans, 16 ouncers, because I didn't have enough money for two six-packs of small cans. Easiest would have been to take some from home, but that was something my parents objected to—I wasn't ever supposed to bring booze out of the house. I think taking beer to a party was too close to their idea of a fraternity bash, which wasn't, of course, social drinking, but only an exercise in mass immaturity. It didn't bother me, because I had a fake ID good enough to fool anyone who wanted to be fooled, like the owner of the tiny grocery store three blocks away from the shopping center. He'd sell anything to anyone who accidentally wandered into his store.

The light flashed green, and I gunned across the intersection, cutting off a little sports jobbie on my right. He was ticked off. I smiled at myself in the mirror. Looking good, I thought. I was in great shape, mellowed out and ready to party, with a few drinks, dinner, and wine down my gullet.

I started to turn at Martha's corner when an explosion hit the trunk of my car like a thunder clap. I slammed on the

16

brakes, and Martha strolled up to the window. "What's the matter, stupid? Can't you recognize your friend?"

"Jeez," I complained. "You didn't have to destroy my car. Was that your fist?"

She went around and got in. "No, it was the flat of my hand. Stings like crazy too. But I had to catch you before you got to my parents. I'm supposedly already over there, supervising decorations or some such bull. I had to figure a way to get the scotch out of the house."

"Right." I'd forgotten about the scotch. "You got it?"

"Sure. I'm saving it all for the party. But I can see you've got a good head start."

"Just my usual," I said. "Can you really tell?" I was surprised, because I felt the same as always, more centered maybe, as if I had the answers to any question I might get asked. Confident. But I didn't think it showed.

Martha's response echoed my thoughts. "You've got that 'I'm the greatest' grin on your face. Your eyes are all bright, and you're real sassy. When you're sober, you brood a lot and keep your mouth shut."

"H-m-m," I mumbled, not sure I liked her answer. "You hear from any colleges yet?"

"Nope. And I better soon, because I'm going to go nuts in one more week if I don't. Watch out for that truck!"

I angled around the truck and rubbed my cheekbone thoughtfully. "I have to take the SAT's next week."

"Yuck! Boy, are they a pain! But you'll do O.K."

It was true I wasn't worried. I'd been on the honor roll every semester since the seventh grade. I felt on top of the world. Champion pitcher, page editor on the paper—I was a hot commodity, all right. At the next light I felt behind me for the beer again. It was still there, as well it should be, unless it had decided to get up and walk off. I'm a little paranoid about losing beer. Then we pulled into Roger's street. "His parents aren't home?" I asked.

"Nope. I wonder how he's squaring this with the neighbors?"

When we got inside, we discovered that Roger's twenty-three-year-old sister was home for a visit and she had agreed to chaperone. Only she was passed out cold in the bathroom.

"Pretty funny," Roger said. "She was making the punch, and she kept tasting it, bigger and bigger swigs, you know. All of a sudden she said she had to pee, and when I went into the bathroom later, there she was, passed out."

Martha and I took charge of that situation, and carried her into the bedroom and tucked her in. She didn't even move. She was totally unconscious. "She must not be used to drinking," I said.

"Either that or too used."

I surveyed the house for hiding places for my beer before I brought it in. I finally decided on the cat food cupboard, figuring no one would think to feed the cat during a drunken brawl. I folded the paper bag tight over the six-pack, now minus the one I had in my hand. I didn't want anyone stealing my beer.

Martha, on the other hand, the big dope, had set her bottle of scotch on the living-room table and was offering it around. A few people took drinks, but most of the party was clustered around the punchbowl in the dining room. Roger's sister had made a fruit juice, rum, and vodka concoction that everybody was guzzling. "It's so sweet," a sophomore said. "Just like candy." Later I saw her puking out the kitchen window.

A couple of kids wanted a blow-by-blow description of Wednesday's game. I was talking when Frank Harris came up and said he had gotten some offers from colleges and ball clubs. "Really?" everybody said. "From who?"

18

"Arizona State and Penn State offered me full scholarships. And the Giants' scouting crew came to watch me pitch last game. They set up an appointment with me and my father next week. And the Cubs have sent me a coupla feelers. I'm waiting to hear—"

I couldn't stand any more. I went to the cupboard, drained the last of my first beer, and extracted another can from the bag. I sat down at the kitchen table. It ticked me off that the boys got all the action, in high school, in college, in the pros. A full scholarship! That must be worth ten thousand, easy. And from what I heard, they got all kinds of bonuses, like a fifty here and there from the loyal alums. Frank didn't even have to go to college. He could sign on for some fat amount with a ball club and play on the farm team awhile. Where would I be? A lousy coed at some lousy college dreaming about my big high school pitching career. Boy, was I important then! Washed up at nineteen. It wasn't that I had anything against Frank, but it—

"Niki?"

"Hi, Frank." I was surprised he still stood there after he saw the look on my face.

"Look," he said, "I saw you walk away, and I realized what a dumb stunt I was pulling, saying all that crap, when you're as good a pitcher as I am, and well . . ."

He was floundering badly, and I finally took pity on him. "I know it's not your fault. It makes me feel lousy, though. It's so unfair."

He watched me as he sat down, as if he were afraid I might suddenly leap up and smite him to the earth. "The only thing I can figure to do about it is support the new law—"

I slapped the table bitterly. "All the new law does is make them bring women's gyms up to standard, the way they should have been already. No extras, I assure you. Nobody's going to offer me a full scholarship, or sign me for a hundred thousand with some pro women's team."

Frank laughed. "Nobody's going to sign me for that kind of money, either," he said. "I'm just a little old Lincoln High pitcher. I might get cut first week in training camp."

"At least you have the option. And you *could* do something, you know. You and a bunch of guys could tell Coach Braxton you want one of the boys' sports cut instead of the softball team."

Frank had a hard time making the mental jump from the Giants' farm club to Lincoln's athletic allocation problems. When he did, he was incredulous. "Cut out one of the boys' sports?"

"Sure," I said. I opened the cupboard and snaked out another beer. "You've got football, basketball, baseball, tennis, swimming, track, even golf, for God's sakes."

"Judy and Teri are on the swim team," he said defensively.

"Big deal. The divers. Maybe you could axe tennis and golf."

Frank stared into the bottom of his punch cup. "Jeez, Niki, two wrongs don't make a right. It's bad to cut out any sport. How 'bout we have a dance and a car wash, or a used book sale, and try to make enough to keep the women's team going? Wouldn't that be better?" He was so pleased with himself, now that he'd saved boys' athletics at good old Lincoln High.

I gulped at my beer and shook my head. "That's cute," I said. "A special dance. Let the ladies go on playing, boys. Cough up a little cash. It might even work."

He looked confused. "I think I'll go get some more punch."

I nodded, engrossed in my own thoughts. "Yeah, right. Hop along, Cass."

He hopped. I laughed. I was feeling cynical. I finished my beer and popped open another. Who cares? Sure, have a car wash! Eliminate one of the teams? Lord, no! And I get to be a cute little coed, dreaming about the teddibly successful car wash, my dear, so I could go on pitching one more year. I laughed again. At least there was booze to keep things in perspective. I figured it was the only thing saving my sanity. It occurred to me a moment later I was getting low on beer. I rummaged in the cat food cupboard. Two more cans. Not much. I looked around. No one. Everybody was still futzing around the punchbowl, and I heard Jimmy begin to play his conga drums. I hated conga drums, but they provided excellent auditory cover to open Roger's parents' refrigerator. I pawed through leftover lettuce and a roast. God, not even wine? What kind of crazy household was this? But then I came up with a prize—three bottles of ale. I glanced over the refrigerator door, and the coast was clear. I grabbed the three bottles and hid them in the cupboard. It was perfect timing, because Sam Shepherd, a drunk of major proportions, chose that moment to come reeling in from the bathroom. Sam and I had traded sarcasms for years, and I could always count on catching his eye during the most ludicrous moments of school pep rallies. "Man," he said, "that punch's almost gone. Old Rog got anything hidden?"

"Don't know," I said disapprovingly, "but whatever is here is his parents'."

"Well, if it offends you that much, Niki, you'd better turn your back." He swung open the refrigerator door and I grinned into my beer can. Surprise of surprises, he found a can of beer I'd overlooked. "One lousy beer," he moaned. "Jesus Christ!"

"Maybe people will stop drinking the punch soon," I said sympathetically.

"Fat chance. They're guzzling in there like a pack of winos. Nobody can get enough. It's dis-gusting!" He swung down into the chair opposite me and propped his chin on one fist. "How come you're sitting in here all alone? Where's that bimbo you used to drag to parties?"

"Are you referring to Chuck?"

"Yeah, that's the dope's name."

I clicked my tongue at him irritably. The only thing Sam was interested in besides staying drunk twenty-four hours a day was chess, and Chuck had been president of the Chess Club last year. The two of them had even traveled together to a regional championship once.

"We broke up over the Christmas holidays." I was sure Sam knew this too.

"Hah! Lucky for you. He's the biggest drag I've ever seen."

I started to get angry, but then I realized this was Sam's clumsy way of trying to make me feel better. He followed up with his inevitable proposition. "I came with Lisa tonight, but since you're footloose and fancy-free . . ." Sam was always suggesting we get together. Neither of us took it seriously. I was concocting a withering remark when a glass shattered in the living room. Roger's voice rose above the tumult, demanding the culprit hide the evidence.

Sam snapped the top off his beer can. "I don't even like parties like this. There's all these amateurs boozing like they know what they're doing. These kids can't handle it the way you and I can." He grinned. I rolled my eyes at him, which signified neither agreement nor disagreement. Sam was one of those people my parents would classify as being in a state of constant poor taste. He was clearly not a social drinker. He even drank in school. I didn't like him lumping us in the same basket, but I also didn't want to be branded as someone who couldn't hold her liquor.

"Where's Lisa anyway?" I asked. It was safest to change the

subject. I didn't like to talk about drinking with Sam.

He jerked his head toward the bathroom in the hall. "In the can. Maybe she passed out."

"Brushing her golden locks," I said.

Sam smiled appreciatively. Lisa's hair was shorter than his. "There she is," he said. "You better get after that punch, Niki, though I see you brought your own supply."

He and Lisa disappeared into the living room. I was glad; I needed another beer, and friends or no, the last thing in the world I'd ever do was open the cat food cupboard in front of Sam.

I circulated while I drank my two remaining beers because I knew I'd have to hide in the kitchen to drink the ale. The brown bottles were a giveaway, and Roger might recognize them as his father's brand or something. Sam was right about the amateur drinking. I would look at people, take a second look, and then realize that girl with the wild eyes was the quiet one from my French class whose voice quivered when she had to answer a question. The dancing was funny too—stagger, stagger, lurch, all across the floor. Roger's sister had woken up, and she seemed to be trying to seduce Andy Lippman, who was embarrassed by that kind of attention from someone older.

Of course, I was pretty ripped by this point. I was standing very stiff and talking very carefully, while people and conversations faded in and out. Then I saw June Sefflin sitting in a corner having an earnest talk with Martha. June's brother had been kicked out of the army on a dishonorable discharge. No one was supposed to know, but naturally everyone had heard immediately. It was never mentioned, in front of June anyway. That was stupid, I thought. Was the army supposed to be a great judge of character? Surely everybody here would look beyond the surface and see how silly the whole thing was. The more I looked at her, the more I realized that she'd been avoiding everybody lately, as if she suspected we knew. I shook my head. Dumb.

I retreated to the kitchen for my ale, but after the first bottle I got lonely, so I figured I'd take a chance. Big deal, anyway. I could always replace them tomorrow before his parents got home. So I swung into the living room, tripped over a foot, and fell sprawling to the floor. "What's the matter with you?" I snarled at Lisa.

"Oh, I'm sorry, Niki," she said, laughing as if near-injuries were hysterical. "You looked so funny."

"Oh, yeah," I said sarcastically. But then I started laughing too. Why hassle? No one should hassle about anything. Life was far too short to tie yourself up in knots over nothing. And that's exactly what June was doing, worrying about something no one cared about. I decided to tell her so.

I strolled up to her and Martha. I was having trouble standing. My body seemed to have a mind of its own. Every time I forgot to stand up straight, I'd start wavering around. "Hey, June," I said. It came out kind of funny. I tried again. "Hey, June. I want to talk to you." There, that was better.

Martha whistled. "Boy, are you ripped. I'm driving home, kiddo, lemme tell ya right now."

"Shut up," I said. "I'm talking to June, not you."

"Well, pardon me, Miss It. I beg your apology, no, that's not right, oh forget it, go ahead."

I noticed June looked like she wanted to be anywhere but here, only I figured once she saw my point of view, she'd be glad. So I launched right in. "I wanted to talk to you about your brother," I announced.

"Niki . . ." Martha said warningly.

"I just wanted to tell you no one cares. The army's a buncha morons, and uh . . ." I ran out of things to say, and somehow it

24

wasn't what I'd thought before. I tried to retrace my little speech, but my mind was too clouded. June looked miserable. A couple of people clapped. "Far out," someone shouted. "About time we talked about it. Go to it, Niki."

This gave me some encouragement. "Who cares what the army thinks? We don't care. None of us, right?" I waved my arm in an expansive gesture and almost fell over.

"'Course we don't care," the same voices shouted. "The army can go bury itself, far as we're concerned."

"Yeah, yeah, that's what I'm trying to say. No one even thinks about it, see?" I finished hopefully, but June's mouth was twisted, as if she were about to cry, and Martha was watching me with this sort of sad, knowing look on her face. "What's the matter with you, Martha?" I yelled at her. "Do you care what the army thinks?"

"No, but I don't think June does either. That's not the point. Why don't you cool it?"

"Ah, screw you," I yelled. "What's the matter with you all of a sudden? I was just trying to—" June took advantage of our argument to slip away, but I didn't notice until I turned to her again. "Where'd she go?" I asked.

"Away from you," Martha answered. "Sit down before you fall down. You're weaving all over the place." She grabbed my arm, but I shook her off. "Gotta get another beer first," I mumbled, and I scrambled away, first to find June, then to get a beer. I stumbled around looking for her, but I was having an awful time walking, and I wasn't too sure what I was doing. I felt as if I was climbing through waves crashing on a shifting beach, and my head was wrapped in a big black cloth that allowed a thought or two to flutter in occasionally. I gave up and went back to the kitchen. Sam was rooting around in the kitchen cabinets with Lisa hanging on his arm.

"Maybe there's some vodka," Lisa said. "I love vodka."

Sam finally found a bottle of brandy. "Here," he said. "Now let's get out of here."

"Gimme a drink first," she said.

"Right, drink first." He opened the bottle and tilted it up to his mouth. I turned my back on them and opened up the cupboard, meanwhile fixing the location of the brandy cabinet in my head. My bottle of ale was still there. I cradled it against my stomach and went toward the living room, bouncing off a couple of walls on the way. Martha looked a long way off, past feet and dozens of bodies. I blinked a few times and finally stuck a finger in front of my right eye. I started walking.

Chapter III

I opened my eyes and closed them and opened them. I was pain. I didn't want to be me. If I could go away ... I waited to fade off, but I started wondering where I was, and that blew it. I looked around. I was in bed, in my room. My Levi's were crumpled on the floor over my shoes. I still wore my shirt and socks. I peered at the clock. Six-forty-two. I kept staring at the clock as if it would tell me if it was morning or night. Finally I realized by the way I felt it had to be morning.

I tried not to panic. I wrapped my arms around myself and hugged, rocking back and forth. "It's O.K., it's O.K.," I whispered, but my mind was on a dark bobsled run all its own. How'd you get home? it screamed. Did you take Martha home? Did you drive? Where's the car? What happened? *What did I do?*

I took deep breaths, trying to make myself settle back into sleep. I couldn't find out the answers until I talked to Martha, and I couldn't call her before eleven. It was a Sunday morning. Eleven was only decent. But how could I find out what happened without letting her know I didn't know? God, what had I done?

I got up and padded to the front door. My car was outside. I went into my room and had to sit on the bed to pull my pants on. I was still drunk. I shouldn't feel this bad if I'm still drunk. I let myself out into the early morning quiet and checked the car. Everything looked all right, no scrapes, no dents. It was parked a little funny, its tail out in the street, meaning I probably drove it home. Jesus! What if I ran over somebody and I don't remember? Ice convulsed my stomach, and I had to grip the door handle to keep from crying out. I *had* to know what happened. I absolutely had to. I would go crazy otherwise. I might have killed someone. I might have done some other horrible thing. My car keys were in my pants pocket. I started the car and took off. After a couple of blocks I realized I was too shaky to drive. I kept clomping on the brakes and then fading out for a few seconds. But I continued on to Martha's. The whole street was quiet, not even a milkman around. My hands were trembling so much I could hardly turn off the ignition. I stepped out and was completely alone.

The grass was slippery, and I walked around the side of Martha's house carefully. I tried to project thought waves against Martha's window, but it didn't work, so I lobbed a pebble up. Smack. Silence. I tried another pebble. Nothing. I went and sat on the curb to wait for Martha to wake up, so I could tackle her immediately. But I got thirsty, and I thought I might faint unless I drank something right away. So I drove home, mixed orange juice, and gulped a quart. My stomach almost revolted, but I massaged it, and the juice stayed down. I tried coffee and the Sunday paper, but I was too busy trying to remember last night to concentrate on the funnies. Jimmy had been playing the conga drums. Did the police come? I had a vague memory of someone in a blue uniform. Then I remembered June, and I dropped my head in my hands. God, what a fool! No one was supposed to know about her brother's dishonorable discharge, and I go babbling on and on. Good intentions maybe, but who cares about intentions when you're being embarrassed by a drunken idiot in front of all your friends? I pushed up from the table and wavered back and forth. Still drunk! I wondered if I was ever going to sober up. I went to my room, took off my clothes, and crawled between the cool sheets. I was framing some kind of apology to June when I fell asleep.

Early morning was as hazy as last night when I woke up again. Had I really driven to Martha's and thrown pebbles at the window? No, I couldn't have. That was crazy. I went out to the kitchen. My parents still weren't awake, and the coffee cup and juice glass sat in the sink. So I had been up. I looked out the front door again at the car. It was parked right. I must have gone to Martha's. I sat down, glanced at the paper, and remembered June again. Oh, no! I seemed to have some sort of compulsion to clear up any tensions when I was drunk, as if we were all one big happy family, no secrets between us friends. I pictured myself staggering around, slurring my words, come on June, everyone knows and no one cares, and her look of fear and disgust. I shivered. What a fool! How could it seem so right then and be so horrible now?

I looked at the clock. Ten-fifteen. Still too early. But then I remembered Martha's eight-year-old brother. Didn't all families with kids get up early? Sure. I dialed the number and Kenny answered on the first ring. "Hauptmanns' residence."

"Hi, Kenny, this is Niki. Martha awake yet?"

"I don't think so. Daddy was mad 'cause she came home so late, and I woke up because everybody was screaming. But nobody's up now. I'm watching cartoons."

"That's nice," I said. "Did you happen to hear, when everybody was screaming, what time it was?"

"Daddy yelled something about three. But you brought her

home, so you know, Niki?" He put a question at the end, so I had to answer.

"Oh, right," I said. "I thought maybe your father hadn't really known if he'd just woken up and didn't look at the time. Then it wouldn't be so bad, see?"

"Yes . . ." he said doubtfully. "I guess."

I heard footsteps and Kenny said, "Oh, here's Martha. Niki's on the phone."

Martha asked Kenny to get her an enormous glass of milk, and I grinned. She was probably pretty out of it too.

"Hi, kid," Martha said. "Didn't expect to hear from you till sundown."

"Bull," I said. "Early bird catches the worm. Well, how'd you like the party?"

"It was a little too crazed for me. You were real funny, racing over the fence to get away from the cops."

I laughed weakly. "Yeah, cops give me the creeps. Did you finish your whole fifth of scotch?" I figured if I asked her enough questions about herself, she'd give me a few clues about what I did.

"Dummy, you did! Don't you remember? You'd finished up your six-pack and a few of those ale things, and then you said you might as well switch to the hard stuff so you could get drunk. I told you you were plenty drunk already, you could hardly walk, but you kept saying, 'Naw, I mean really drunk, fly me to the moon,' and that sort of trash. There was about a quarter of the bottle left, which you finished off. That was even after you did your cute trip with June. You remember that? About ten people left when you launched into your tirade."

"Oh."

"That was really blown, Niki. It's none of your business."

I closed my eyes and tried to think. "Maybe you should have dragged me away or knocked me out."

"Oh, sure! You have no idea how obnoxious you get when you're drunk. You act like you're the king of the mountain and everybody else is some kind of stupid serf. And you're belligerent too. Do you remember trying to punch Marci Gainler?"

"Marci Gainler?" I echoed.

"I'm not sure what happened, but I think she said something to you about the team, like we were going to have a harder time this year. A moment later you were swinging at her. Frank dragged you outside and sat on you. I went out and he left, and you started crying about fish or the ocean or something. I couldn't tell what, since you were almost incoherent."

"I started crying?" I said. I couldn't believe it. I hadn't cried since I was eleven, not to my knowledge anyway.

"Oh, yeah. About crabs. I couldn't tell what was the matter with you. About that time the police came, and you got it together, thank God, and dragged me over the back fence, and we went through yards to get to the car. How's your head?"

"Head? What about it?"

"You tripped on a root and fell against a brick wall. You were bleeding last night."

"Wait a minute," I said. I went into the bathroom, remembering that I hadn't looked at myself yet. On my forehead was a scrape crusted with dried blood. And dirt. And red-rimmed eyes. I looked awful. Puffy and bloody. I washed my face off, and it wasn't as bad as it looked. Just a scrape.

"It's nothing much," I reported when I got back to the phone.

"Well, it looked horrible last night. You don't remember too much, do you?"

"No," I admitted. "I vaguely remember talking to June. I'm

not sure what I said. I remember going to get another ale. And that's it. I don't remember Marci or crying or the fence or anything else."

"Isn't that a little weird? That never happened to me."

"Oh, no," I said. "It happens all the time when you're really drunk. The first time Roger got drunk, he woke up in the middle of town in an alley, and the last thing he remembered was sitting at home watching a game on TV."

"Hm-m-m. I wonder why it doesn't happen to me."

"I don't know."

Silence. I figured Martha hated me, and she had good reason to. I didn't want to continue to be obnoxious, but I had to know. "Martha," I said finally, "are you angry at me?"

Martha thought while I fidgeted. If she had to think that long . . . "No," she said finally. "But I'd rather not be with you if you're going to get that drunk. Understand?"

"Oh, sure," I said, relieved. "I'll be careful next time."

"Good," Martha said, and she sounded relieved too. "What was all that stuff about fish and crabs?"

My face flushed, and I was glad she was on a phone and not in front of me. "I can't imagine. Drunken ravings. Listen, I'm going to shower. I'll see you later."

"Right."

We broke off, and I drank some more orange juice and went back to bed.

Chapter IV

"And, unfortunately, after every Sunday comes a Monday
..." I was singing in the shower, trying to keep up my spirits. I
didn't want to go to school at all. I was still too embarrassed.
What if I saw June? Or Marci? And there was the scrape on
my forehead, making it obvious to everybody that I'd blown it
somehow or other.

I got out of the shower, toweled myself down, and tried to
arrange my hair so it would cover the scrape. It sort of worked.
You'd have to look hard to see it. I thought about staying home
sick, but everybody might think I was still hung over. I decided to go and try to act normal. After all, everybody at the party was drunk. At least I didn't puke like that sophomore, and
Sam even stole a bottle of brandy. I shouldn't have much to
worry about.

But as I parked the car, my stomach knotted up, and I
glanced at the crowd on the steps. No kids from the party. I
hoisted myself out, locked the door, and literally ran down the
hall to my first class, keeping my face straight ahead, as
though I were on some life or death mission. It wasn't until I'd
opened the door that I remembered Marci was in my English

class. Luckily she wasn't there yet. I strode to my seat, responding curtly to people's greetings, acting as if I was preoccupied.

A moment later Marci walked in and her eyes flew right to me. I nodded carefully in her direction. She blinked at me and sat down. I sighed, wishing it was tomorrow, or better yet, the next day. It wouldn't be so bad then.

I spent all of English trying to devise a story to explain the scrape on my head. My parents had believed a garbled version of the truth: Martha and I had discovered Roger's parents didn't know about the party, and we had decided to leave. But suddenly the police rushed in, and we went out the back door so we wouldn't be arrested and cause a hassle. "Bad publicity," I'd said sanctimoniously, and my parents had agreed. They were sorry, though, that I'd cracked my head on a fence.

That story wouldn't work with Scotty. She knew Martha and I wouldn't leave a party for such moral reasons. In fact, Scotty would probably think the only way we'd leave a party was to get thrown out. I was no closer to a solution by the time I got to P.E., and Scotty, of course, noticed immediately.

"What'd you do to your head?" she asked. She pushed away my hair for a better look.

"Fell on it," I said gruffly.

Scotty narrowed her eyes at me. "Just fell?"

"Uh-huh." I smiled. She shook her head.

Martha collared me at the lockers. "Did you talk to June?"

"No. I haven't seen her." This was truthful, but it was because I'd spent the day looking at no one, and I'd left campus for lunch and hidden in the bathroom or the library whenever I had any free time. So I really hadn't seen anyone but Marci.

"I did see Marci," I reported.

"What happened?"

I shrugged. "Nothing. We said hello."

"Hm-m. She's a lot nicer than I'd be under the circumstances. How do you feel?"

"I feel fine, Martha," I said irritably. "I got drunk. It's no big deal."

"You didn't sound that way yesterday. You sounded pretty freaked."

"That's because I was hung over."

I'd finished dressing, so I ran out to cut the conversation off. I didn't want to tell her how embarrassed I was. It was dumb. Every single person at that party was staggering around all over the place. I warmed up my arm with Teri, trying to understand why I felt so guilty. I couldn't forget the image of myself weaving over June, slurring my words, while everybody laughed. I've gotta pull myself together, I thought. Go down to Carmel and look at the ocean.

After practice, Scotty called me into her office.

"Well?" I said, not able to meet her eyes. I figured she knew I was drunk, and I braced myself for some blow.

Scotty sent her hand through her short blond hair like a homing pigeon. Her finger scratched an ear. She only did that when she was nervous, and my feeling of foreboding grew. Today was definitely a bummer, avoiding people, Scotty acting weird . . .

"Martha tells me you hurt your head when you were drunk," Scotty said finally.

"Oh, yeah?" I snapped. Instant anger surged up in hot red waves and wiped out any warning voices. "What's that to you?" I was shocked at myself, but I didn't let my face show it. I glared at her as if she was my persecutor.

She retreated; her eyes tightened defensively. "Not much, I guess. But if you ever want to talk about it?"

I squelched the hope in her voice. "What's there to talk about? I got drunk and hit my head, right? Millions of people do it every day." I started to leave, but Scotty's voice made me pause at the door. I didn't turn around.

"I don't mean this incident in particular, Niki. I meant if you wanted to talk about your drinking in general."

"I just got drunk," I repeated, and I walked out. The locker room was empty, end-of-school desolation, and I paced between the banks of lockers until I reached the bench farthest from Scotty's office. I sat down, squeezing my hands into fists to keep them from trembling. Who did she think she was talking to? She was supposed to be my friend. And Martha! I wanted to kill them both. I'm the star pitcher on their softball team, and they treat me as if I'm some helpless old drunk that they pity. I gritted my teeth and dug my nails into the palms of my hands until the hurt got to me. Nobody, nowhere, was *ever* going to pity me! I'd kill them or kill me first. I decided I couldn't see them anymore, either of them. But that would mean I'd have to quit the team. How could they do this to me? I didn't want to quit the team. No, I'd stay on, just not talk to them. I wasn't some dumb punk they could push around. I could take anything they threw at me. I could take anything anyone threw at me. They'd see.

When Martha called that night at her usual time, I answered on the first ring. "Martha?" I said, before she'd had a chance to say anything.

"Yeah? What's—"

"What're you trying to pull, Martha? I don't want you messing with me, with my life, with anything, understand? Leave me alone!" I flung the phone back on the receiver, and I stared at the wall, horribly unhappy, all alone. I wanted to die. Martha was my best friend. How could she betray me?

I went into my room and got out a book I'd hidden behind the radio. I'd stolen it one day when I was at the university bookstore. I spent a lot of time on the Berkeley campus, even before Chuck started college there. I liked to prowl around the bookstores and the coffeehouses; the school's business fringe started only half a mile from our house.

The book was a little paperback called *Alcohol Dependence*. I turned to the part on blackouts, the part I'd read a million times. "Although occasionally normal drinkers have blackouts," it read, "a blackout, or complete loss of memory while drinking, must be considered a serious sign of trouble. In chronic alcoholics, blackouts increase in frequency until sometimes whole weeks are lost to the drinker. A heavy, non-alcoholic drinker may experience one or two blackouts during a career of drinking. But anyone having a history of blackouts, especially with a change of personality while drinking, should consider that he or she has crossed the invisible line into alcoholic drinking."

I read it again, and then I put the book down, shaking my head. I couldn't be an alcoholic. I was only seventeen. Alcoholics could never drink only one beer. I could, especially if I had a hangover. I never drank in the morning, or at school, the way Sam did. But I had been having blackouts. In fact, I blacked out the first time I got drunk, when I was fourteen. So actually then the book had to be wrong. Weren't blackouts a cumulative effect? Maybe the book was too old, and there were new studies. Or I might be more sensitive than most people. What if I was allergic to alcohol? But wasn't that alcoholism? I stopped trying to think, stuck the book back behind the radio, and began to do my chemistry homework. I was too restless to study. I could call Martha— Oh, right, I wasn't speaking to Martha. I dropped my head in my hands. I felt so lonely.

I wish I was grown up. I wish I was twenty-one, in college. I wouldn't be so nervous if I wasn't living with my parents and going to high school. That was why I drank all the time. You had to stay sane some way. High school would drive anyone to drink. There was so damn much pressure. SAT's on Saturday morning, for instance. All this trash about these being the best years was so much bull.

If these were the best years, I might as well shoot myself now, because things couldn't get much worse. What I needed was a vacation. Carmel, all by myself. That would be good. Better if Martha came. But— Oh, I can't stand this!

I snatched up the phone and dialed Martha's number quickly before I changed my mind. She answered herself. "Martha?"

"Niki?"

"Listen," I said, "I'm sorry I yelled at you."

"Well, I'm sorry too. I was worried, and I thought maybe Scotty could help. She said she was going to talk to you. I'm *still* worried."

"There's nothing to worry about," I insisted. "I told you I'd be careful next time. I won't drink so much, that's all."

"But Niki, you don't remember drinking the scotch. You kept wanting to get drunker when you were practically unconscious. How can you make sure it won't happen if you don't even know you're doing it?"

"I won't get so drunk I don't know what I'm doing again. You'll see. Let me handle this."

"All right, Niki. Have you thought about the game with Ridgedale yet?"

"Yes. Their first baseman is a real maniac. She's a fighter."

"You don't have to tell me that. I got into a brawl with her when I subbed in as a sophomore. She was a soph then too. I hope you don't bean her or anything. She'd kill you."

"Don't worry about me, kiddo. Just worry about yourself standing there on the bag. She messed up Francie's leg—you know the one on St. Ignatius' team? She shoved Francie right off the base and sprained her leg for her."

"That's nice," Martha mused. "And then there's that short-stop, what's her name . . ."

By the time we hung up, an hour later, we were best friends again, and I went to bed happy. Everything was going to be all right. All I had to do was be careful. Maybe if I drank a lot of milk it would coat my stomach.

Chapter V

The day of the game, Scotty called me into her office again. "Can you play?" she asked. I stared at her. "Why couldn't I?" I said.

"I don't know. I just wondered if you could. You look sort of tired."

"I'm fine," I snapped. I went back to my locker and put on my shoes with the rubber cleats.

Martha sat down beside me. "You see the game on TV last night?"

"Yeah. It was pretty good."

Martha examined me carefully. "*You* don't look good."

"I got drunk while I was watching the game. I'm a little hung. I'll be all right."

"O.K. Did you lose your memory?"

I shook my head. "It's called a blackout."

"Oh. How'd you know that?"

"What?" I said irritably.

"Blackout. How'd you—"

"Everybody knows that, Martha." I turned away from her

fast and trotted out to the field. Why had I told her that? Get it together, stupid, I yelled at myself.

Sarah hadn't arrived yet, so I practiced pitching to one of the outfielders. Where was Sarah? I was in a thoroughly bad mood, especially since Scotty was hassling me. Whenever I had a hangover, I felt like four layers had been peeled off my skin, and I was too sensitive to touch, too quick to anger. Everything bad had happened to me already, and nothing I did would make it worse.

Sarah finally emerged from the gym. She waved off the outfielder and started strapping on her equipment. "Watch out for Julie Baxter," she said.

"Who's she?"

"Their first baseman."

"I know about her. You want to practice throwing to second? I'm tired. I'm going to sit down for a while."

I realized I should have skipped journalism and lunch and gone out to the car and slept for two hours. I was exhausted. I slumped down in the dugout and put my head on my arms. A moment later I heard a voice at my side. "I'm going to have Alice warm up," Scotty said. Alice was the sophomore relief pitcher.

"I tell you I'm all right!" I flared. "I'll be fine once the game starts."

And I was, at least for the first three innings. In fact, my sense that nothing mattered seemed to help my pitching. I wasn't nervous. I took more chances, and a lot of them worked. I struck out the side in the third inning. While we hustled to the dugout, Martha grabbed my arm. "Niki, you're pitching better than I've ever seen. Maybe you oughta get drunk before every game."

"Maybe," I said. "It does seem to help." But exhaustion was

flooding through me, and whenever we were off the field, I collapsed. Our lead was only three runs, not really comfortable. I had to keep up, but I wasn't sure I'd be able to.

Their pitcher was no slouch. She retired us quickly, one hit, no runs. I went back out on the mound and faced the top of their order. I stalled around a little, but I had to start sometime, so I fired a fastball across the plate. The girl swung, looked surprised at the skidding ball, and took off down the first-base line. Ginny made a bad throw to first. Martha couldn't hold on to it. She recovered the ball right away, but the girl was already sliding into second. I shook my head. God, I wish I wasn't so tired!

We got up to a full count on the next batter, and in a fit of sheer nervous energy I struck her out. And then Julie Baxter was up. She sneered at me and spat into the dirt at her feet. I snorted, grinning at Martha. "Hot stuff," I yelled to her.

"The hottest," Martha said sarcastically.

I floated in my sinker, and she fell for it, swinging much too high. "Strike one!" the umpire bawled. Julie stepped out of the box, crouched down, and dug out a little hole for her lead foot. I amused myself by feinting at the woman on second. Then I threw a lousy pitch, high and outside. Julie grinned.

"Good eye, good eye," all the creeps on her team shouted. I was inside next pitch, but the ump called it a strike, and we had a minute break while Julie screamed and argued. Without thinking, I lobbed the ball to Martha, and the girl on second took off. Martha made a good throw, but she had to throw over me, since I didn't duck. The girl made it standing. "Oh, damn!" I said miserably.

Martha trotted over. "Hey, silly, whatsa matter with you?"

"I don't know. I forgot she was there."

"Uhm-hm." Martha patted me on the arm. "Don't worry.

You'll strike out this turkey, and the one up after her hits flies ninety percent of the time. Don't lose your cool."

But I had. I couldn't believe I'd done something so stupid in the middle of a game. I could hear the other team laughing at me from the dugout. Julie was finally ready, and I threw a fast pitch that missed completely. And then I spun one in desperately, eager only to hit the strike zone, and Julie hit a long ball to center that the fielder had to chase. I watched the woman on third trot across the plate while Julie tore around second. "Come on!" I yelled. Teri had moved way out on the outfield grass to take the relay throw from center. She fired it home, but the ball was off target. Julie didn't hesitate a moment at third. I ran to home plate while Sarah grabbed the ball off the first-base line. I could hear Julie's feet pounding, and I stood crouched, my foot on the plate, ready to spin for the tag. The ball hit my glove, I turned, and Julie plowed into me, her arms outstretched. I flew against the backstop, and I was up in a second. "What the fuck you think you're doing?" I yelled.

"Get outta my way next time, ya stupid creep!" she shouted.

I threw down the ball and the glove and my mind snapped to some other place. I hurled myself at her, and we were on the plate, in the dirt, my hands wrapped around her throat. I raised one fist and smashed her in the face, and she grabbed my arm and spun me over, jamming her knee into my stomach. A second later Sarah and Martha had dragged me off. I was coughing, spitting dirt out of my mouth. "You're out," the umpire shouted at Julie. Then she turned to me. "And you're out of the game!"

"What?" I screamed. "You can't do that! She—"

Scotty ran over, grabbed my arm, and told me to go to the gym right away. "Go on," she said. "We'll talk about this later."

"That's crazy!"

Martha twisted my arm. "Niki, get out of here. But wait at the gym. I want you to drive me home. All right?"

The mention of driving home brought my head back. "Oh, yeah," I said. "All right."

I left, the other team's cheers ringing in my ears, and I hoped Alice could keep it together. I showered, lay down on the bench, and fell asleep in about ten seconds.

I started awake when I heard the clatter of equipment and voices. It took me a moment to remember what happened, and when I did I put my head back on the bench. Playing possum. I was behind some lockers. I wanted to hear if we had won or lost. I didn't want to think about the fight yet.

Martha crashed down on the bench beside me. "Figured you'd stay around," she said.

I kept my mouth shut. I wanted her to tell me the score, not make a big thing out of it. "We lost," she said heavily. "Wasn't Alice's fault. She did O.K. Our hitting was a disaster." She bent to untie her shoes, and a minute later, she was standing naked in front of me. I watched the sweat roll between her high breasts. "Scotty wants to see you. I'll be in the shower."

I walked between the rows of lockers. The jetting water from the showers sounded like an ocean, but it seemed quiet to me. No yelling, no horseplay. It was the first game we'd lost in a while. Nobody had ever been thrown out of a game, not in my memory at least, except maybe Julie. I felt awful.

Scotty's door was open. Her back was turned, and smoke from her little cigarette wound around her like a wreath. I rapped on the door frame.

She swiveled to face me, and I saw the lines etched around her eyes. "I hope you're not still pretending you're the Lone Ranger," she said.

I sat down. "No, I feel like a fool. I hear we lost."

"That's right. But it wasn't Alice's fault."

Her words hung in the air. It was obvious whose fault it was. "That's what Martha said," I answered obliquely. Scotty twisted a pencil around in her fingers. "You weren't in shape, mentally or physically, for this game."

"No," I admitted. "But I pitched O.K. while I was in."

Scotty nodded. "That's because you happen to be an excellent softball pitcher, one of the best I've ever seen. But you would have fallen apart. You were playing on guts and that only lasts so long. I was going to pull you out after that inning, even before you threw the ball away to Martha. My big mistake was letting you play at all. Your reactions were shot. If someone had smashed a ball right at your head, I'd probably have a dead pitcher on my hands instead of a hungover one."

I wasted a little time trying to figure out which she'd rather have. I mumbled something. She ignored me. "I've thought a lot about what to do, Niki. There are several alternatives. I could point out to you that you're in training and forbid you to drink altogether, but I think it's stupid to make rules I don't enforce and you won't follow. I don't want to suspend you, because the team needs you, and this is the first time this has happened at a game. But you have been hung over at practices, sometimes severely. So what I've decided to do is leave it up to you, with the warning that if you come to a game, a practice, or a wrap-up meeting hung over or drunk, you're off this team. Understand?"

I nodded and got up to leave. "O.K.," I said. "See you tomorrow." I could feel her eyes boring into my back as I walked out the door. I knew she wanted me to talk to her about it, but what could I say? O.K., I'd done a stupid thing. That was the end of it.

I figured out the days as I was walking to the car. We had full-fledged practices Mondays and Fridays, and Thursday was wrap-up day. And of course, we played on Wednesday. Which means, I thought, that I can only drink Monday night. And Friday and Saturday. Well, that's three nights a week. Oughta be plenty for anybody. But the middle of the week loomed in front of me like a big desert. It meant I couldn't drink tonight, for instance. I really wanted a beer. Who cared about wrap-up? We didn't even hit the field. But then again, she'd just said hung over, and so hung over that she'd recognize it at two in the afternoon. That was easy. I'd drink only beer tonight, no hard stuff, not even wine.

Martha was sitting on the curb next to the car. "God, I'm sorry," I said. "I forgot it was locked. I should have given you the key."

"That's O.K.," Martha said, getting up and stretching. "What'd Scotty say?"

"She says I can't be hung over at any game, practice, or wrap-up. Or I'm off." I eliminated drunk, since that would never happen anyway. Weird she even mentioned it.

Martha hopped in the car. "Let's see. That means you can't drink Tuesday, Wednesday, or Thursday nights. And Sunday. Wow. That'll be hard. You think you can do it?"

"Of course I can do it," I said. "You and Scotty act like I'm some kind of alcoholic or something. Anyway, it's just for two months."

"Yeah, that's true. You want to get some ice cream?"

"Naw, ice cream's too sweet for me. I'm going home and get a beer."

"But, Niki, tomorrow's—"

"She said hung over, Martha. I'm not going to get hung over on one beer. And I don't want you bugging me about it."

"O.K., O.K., Niki."

We drove on in silence. Martha didn't call me that night. I think she didn't want to be checking on me.

Chapter VI

Luckily I didn't have to go into a big explanation of my new drinking schedule to my parents. We were still embroiled in the great Tax Crisis. My father and I spent our hours home tiptoeing around the house, whispering to each other in the kitchen while we searched the shelves for something other than the case of cream of celery soup my mother won once in a bingo game. One evening, after I'd finished my homework and my father had read the paper twice, we both gratefully collapsed in the TV room, where we could make a little more noise, since it was at the opposite end of the house from the downstairs study. "Isn't this a little insane?" I asked Carl.

He peered at me over the top of the *TV Guide*. "Isn't what a little insane, Niki?"

"This hysteria over the taxes. The more time she supposedly spends keeping up on it during the year, the worse it actually is in April. I don't remember her doing this when I was younger." My father was reading the *Guide;* he probably hadn't heard a word I'd said. That was O.K., because I had figured out her motives while I was talking and I wanted to think about it. I realized Joyce needed to prove her worth to Carl,

47

and doing all the money stuff was the only way she could think of to do it. She hadn't made a big deal out of the taxes until I was around thirteen, because before that she'd been a full-time mother. We'd all had our jobs: I was being a kid, Joyce was being my mother, and Carl was the father and the breadwinner. Now I was a student, Carl was still the breadwinner, and my mother became the bookkeeper.

My father had made his choice from the *TV Guide*. He levered himself off the couch and tuned in some dumb situation comedy. I watched him, thinking about parents in a new way. My parents had picked each other, not been inexorably linked from birth, as children tend to believe. They both still had stuff to prove to each other, an entirely separate relationship to maintain, a bond less stable than the one they had with me. I'd always be their daughter, but they wouldn't always necessarily be married. The thought creeped me out and made me realize why Chuck had wanted such a tight thing with me. Sometimes going with him seemed like being in prison. But he had needed something secure to replace what he'd lost when his parents divorced the year before.

I sighed and tried to focus on the TV show. It was too stupid. If this was what they thought teenagers wanted to watch, they oughta go ask a few. I really did try to concentrate on the show, but I kept thinking about my mother. It was more obvious now why she didn't like me as a teenager. Nothing I did satisfied her. Her little bird had stretched its wings and flown away, but it was still unaccountably coming back around the nest to grab food. She didn't know what to do with me, so she fell back on molding me into her image of the perfect young lady, which I stubbornly refused to fit. Playing softball, for one thing. That was dumb. Breaking up with Chuck had been a big mistake. I wasn't sociable enough. I didn't dress right. Sure, my grades were good, but that was expected. It made me feel lonely, because while my mother was immersed in her idea of what I should be, she'd lost sight of who I was.

My father, on the other hand, was vastly relieved I was older. I'd noticed he was uncomfortable around children. Maybe he thought they were boring or dumb. He started shepherding me into adulthood right away. He was always telling people how sensible I was. The way he reacted when I mentioned not drinking was typical Carl. All I said was I was swamped with work and had to study in the middle of the week. At first he didn't see what that had to do with cocktail hour or dinner wine, but then he caught on. "Oh, I understand. You want to be sharp for your work. Sure, Niki. If I have to prepare something for the morning, I always lay off the night before. Good thinking." He was proud of me. He said I was the most grown-up teenager he knew.

Well, he was right, I thought. I really was growing up, starting to see my parents as real people. It made me sad for my mother. I couldn't help getting older, or that I wasn't turning out the way she wanted. But I could stop riding her so much. What a bummer she felt she had to be the bookkeeper! Maybe my father could . . . "Say, Carl. I was thinking about this tax stuff."

He dragged his eyes off the tube for one split second. "Forget it. Joyce just likes to make mountains out of molehills."

I was disappointed, but eventually I did forget it. I had enough problems of my own. Both Martha and Scotty watched me out of the corners of their eyes that first week, but they stopped after I seemed to be handling it all well. Stuff at school settled down. My only hassle was drinking more on the nights I could drink, as if I'd signed a pact with myself to get as drunk as possible. There were more little papers in my typewriter in the mornings. Monday nights were the worst, since I had that long dry period to live through until Friday. "This schedule business is really bad for my drinking," I told Martha. "If there weren't any restrictions, I'd drink fine. All these rules are screwing things up."

"You yourself said it was only for two months."

"True." But two months seemed like an eternity, especially Wednesdays after the games. I'd always drink a few beers, and the second week I drank a little more than I could hide the next day. I snuck in the gym on my lunch period, showered, squirted red-out in my eyes, and chewed a bunch of mints. I probably ended up looking fresher than anybody by the time we had the wrap-up.

Week three, after the taxes were finally done, some friends of my parents' came to visit. We took them out to dinner Sunday night. I knew it would be crude to order beer as a cocktail, so I ordered a gin and tonic and thought I'd sip it. When they were on their third drink, I gave up and got my second. And then wine. My father was in his glory, discussing the possible choices with the wine steward. We talked about the economy all during dinner, which might seem indigestible, but it drove high school and pitching clear to the back of my mind. The last thing I wanted to be was a high school student, pitcher or not. It was stupid, for kids. We drove home, and everybody suddenly wanted to play pool. There was nothing to do but go to the local pool hall. We all ordered beers, and I was shooting pretty well for once. And then back home for more beer, and we organized a poker game. When I woke up, I knew I'd blown it. Really blown it. I could hardly get out of bed. The quart of orange juice almost didn't stay down. I thought about staying home sick, but I had a big chemistry test, and they'd have to arrange a makeup if I didn't take it. And—well, it was stupid. The whole thing was stupid. Who cared about softball anyway? Besides, I could just shower and do my red-out and mint routine. I tripped off to school.

50

After English and chemistry, I was really dragging. The test had gone O.K., but in math I sobered up enough to realize how bad off I was. My hands were shaking as if I had Parkinson's disease. I wasn't thinking clearly. I skipped U.S. history and went to first period lunch. I drank about a gallon of milk, hoping that would help. I needed to sleep. That was it. I started out to the car, and met Martha coming down the block. "Hey," I said. "How'd you get out of Miner's class?"

"She sent me to the office to get something. While they're finding it, I thought I'd go have a smoke. What's the matter with you? You— Niki, you're real messed up, hunh?"

I nodded. "I was going to the car to sleep it off. I hope." I explained about the out-of-town visitors.

"Did you black out?"

"Yeah. I don't remember going to bed. I was still drunk this morning. I took the chem test half swacked, but I think I did pretty well. It's wearing off now, though, and I feel horrible."

Martha leaned close and sniffed. "You smell horrible too," she reported. "You smell like a brewery. You must be sweating it out. What are we going to do?"

I was both pleased and irritated that Martha considered this her problem too. I wished I could think sensibly. My brain seemed to be running around in tight little circles and I couldn't focus on anything without drifting off. "I mostly need to sleep," I said. Just saying it made me incredibly weak, and I stumbled.

Martha grabbed my arm. "Come on," she said. She led me to the car, opened the door, and shoved me in the back seat. "I'll wake you up ten minutes before the bell. I can get out of art easy. Then you can run down and shower. Will you be O.K.?" She was worried, and I suddenly wanted to be alone.

"Yeah, yeah," I said, waving her away. "I just need to sleep." I settled back, but it was uncomfortable, and my head wouldn't stop thinking about horrible things, like severed arms and dogs being run over. I wondered if I was going insane. At least Scotty couldn't blame me if I went insane and couldn't pitch. But I didn't want to go insane. Why were there all these pressures? I felt sick, really sick. I leaned out of the car and threw up all the milk I'd drunk. That was better, I thought, resting back, but then my head started running again, and I knew I'd scream if it didn't stop.

There was no way this was going to work. I got out of the car and started walking around aimlessly, knowing I should be asleep and hassling myself about it every step. Behind the school, deep in the weeds of the vacant lot, I heard voices. Probably smoking dope, I thought. I made a face. I didn't like a dope high. But on the other hand, it might make my hangover go away, or at least let me sleep. I started toward the voices.

"Who's there?" A challenge. Sam's voice.

"It's me, Niki. What's going on?" I shoved some huge weeds aside.

"Just havin' a taste, Niki, old kid. Come on over."

I stumbled into the circle of beaten-down weeds, and Sam waved a bottle of vodka at me. He was with a sophomore who was supposed to be a hot lineman on the junior varsity.

"Here, have some," Sam said when I'd sat down.

I waved it away. "No, I've got a hangover that won't quit."

"Well, this'll make it better."

"The idea makes me puke."

"Sure it does now," Sam explained. "But I guarantee ya, it'll get rid of that hangover faster than anything. Ya got the shakes?"

I held out my hands for inspection. They quivered all over the place.

"That's plain crazy, Niki!" Sam said. "You don't need to feel like that!" He shoved the bottle in my face, and I took a big swig.

I immediately turned and retched on the grass. "Won't work," I coughed. "The smell alone makes me sick." I was embarrassed that I'd vomited in front of them, but neither seemed to care.

"That always happens," Sam said. "Sometimes it takes two or three tries before it stays down."

I swallowed out of the bottle again, and kept it down, but it just made my headache worse. "It's no good," I said. I tried to hand him back the bottle, but he wouldn't take it.

"Go on. Take a big swallow." I did, and then another. My nose was all scrunched up, like I was taking medicine. Then another swallow. Sam grabbed the bottle out of my hand. "Ya don't have to drink it all, ya know."

"Oh, yeah, sorry," I said.

I leaned back, and my head cleared up. I felt good all of a sudden. The shakes were gone. "Hey, you were right. I feel O.K."

"Sure, told ya."

"Hey, Sam," the kid said. "Hey, Sam, kin we get another bottle before lunch's over? She drank half of this one."

"Oh, come on," I said. "Two gulps. Besides, can't you think for yourself?"

"He's got the ID," the kid said sullenly.

"Here, use mine. Says I'm twenty-two."

The kid reached out his hand and then snatched it back. "You're a girl," he said.

I laughed. "Really? Gee, I must have forgotten there for a minute."

Sam grinned at me. "Look, Jeff, the bell's about to ring. You go on now. I'll meet ya here tomorrow, but don't forget the three bucks."

"Yeah, tomorrow," he said, and he shambled off through the weeds.

"What's this about three bucks?" I asked.

But Sam was digging around in his jacket pocket. He produced a full pint and waved it triumphantly. "Hah!" he chortled. "The three? Well, he pays me three for half of a half-pint each lunch. I make enough profit to buy a pint for myself every week. Just a little extra dividend."

"Sharp," I said. "Very sharp." I watched him open the bottle, and we both drank deeply. But when he handed it back to me, I shook my head. "Nope, I've got practice later."

He shrugged. "All the more for me. Say, you booze it up with your parents, hunh?"

"I wouldn't call it boozing it up," I said irritably. "We have cocktails together in the evening."

Sam snickered. "That's what I thought. I'm going to tell my parents that when they ask me why I can't get on the honor roll every time like you do. I'll just say, 'Niki Etchen has cocktails in the evening. She doesn't have to drink all day at school like some people I know.' "

"Brilliant," I said sarcastically. I sat while he drank, and then I reached out my hand again. He grinned and unloosened the bottle. "Hey, Niki!" he said suddenly, as if he'd thought of something really stupendous. "You wanta ball?"

"No."

"How come?"

"How come you always ask me when you're drunk?"

He pursed his lips. "I don't know. Guess it's the only time I think of it."

"Maybe that's why," I said.

We drank in silence. I think I fell asleep for a few minutes. School was far away, though we could make out people moving in the building above us.

"Hey, what time is it?"

Sam lazily looked at his watch. "Twenty after three. You gotta go?"

"Damn! My practice started ten minutes ago." I jumped up and reeled back against a tree. "Oh, no! I'm drunk!"

"No kidding?" Sam said.

"I can't go to practice like this."

"No kidding."

"Probably better anyway," I said, leaning on the tree trunk. "I'll tell Scotty I have cramps or something. She can't complain about that."

I felt amazingly clear-headed, but my body wouldn't do anything I wanted it to. It was pretty funny. I could see why Sam drank in school. It made it bearable. Especially, I thought, giggling, when you didn't even go. But this was the last time, I told myself. One little fall from grace, and back up on the straight and narrow after today. I sat down and reached for the bottle again.

"All gone," Sam said, holding it upside down.

"Ah, what a shame!" Even the bottle being empty was funny. I giggled again, but I stopped when I felt Sam's arm around me, his hand clawing at my breasts.

"Cut it out," I said.

"Aw, come on, Niki. I gave ya all that free booze!"

"Forget it!" We wrestled around in the weeds, and I started getting scared when I realized how much stronger he was. But I managed to catch him a good one with my foot, and he grabbed at his knee. I was up and running, or up and staggering is more like it, and I darted behind a tree. I had to slam my hand over my mouth to keep from laughing. I could hear him crashing around in the weeds. When he got close, I broke from cover, leapt down an embankment, and hid in a tall clump of trees. I was pretending I was a goddess escaping from a particularly horny god. It was fun. Sam was laughing by this time. We raced around and around the lot, throwing dirt clumps at each other, and then the final bell pealed across the field.

"I've gotta go," I said. "Martha'll want a ride home."

"Hey," he said, panting, "tell Martha for me that I'll give her a ride home sometime. I like her. I mean, I'm interested in her."

"Oh," I said and paused. I knew he was serious this time. "O.K., I'll tell her." But he'd heard my voice go flat.

"Why're you actin' like that? Hunh?"

"You know, Sam, she—"

"Because I drink? Is that what you were going to say? You're her best friend, right? She can't mind drunks too much. Hunh? Right?" He pointed a long dirty index finger at me, and I shook my head, not sure why I was shaking it.

"I gotta go," I said, and I took off through the weeds.

I flopped into the driver's seat just as Martha turned the corner. The half-hour running around had sobered me up a little, but not much. "Where were you?" Martha asked as she climbed in beside me. "I looked all over."

"I was in the vacant lot," I said.

"In the lot? You're drunk!"

"Just a little. See, I thought it'd make my hangover go away, and it did, only I was bored, so I drank too much, and I forgot what time it was, so I missed practice, but I figure it's better anyway because—"

"Shut up!" Martha shouted. "God, you're such an idiot, Niki! What's the matter with you?"

I was flabbergasted. "What do you mean?"

"You were so hung over this morning you could hardly walk, and now you're so drunk you can hardly walk." Martha's voice was shaking. "You must have a big thing about not walking, huh? And it's the middle of the afternoon. Not that it matters."

"You're not making much sense," I said. I was scared. She was so freaked out. "What are you so upset about? God, so I got drunk."

"I'm upset because I'm your friend. I like you. Hell, I even love you. You keep telling me you just got drunk, no big deal, you can handle everything, don't worry, Martha, and you keep getting worse! You're getting worse!"

I thought she was going to cry. If she did, I would too, even though I couldn't understand what we were going to cry about. I reached out for her hand. "Martha, I—"

"Forget it! Come on, take me home."

I pulled out into the traffic and drove fairly carefully, sneaking glances at Martha every once in a while. I didn't know what to think, and I didn't know how to make things better. "I have been following Scotty's orders," I said finally. "For a whole month."

Martha didn't answer. She kept staring out the window. I pulled up at her house and jammed on the parking brake. "You're home," I said.

She turned around, and her eyes were full of tears. I reached out for her again, but she pulled back. "I told Scotty you had your period. I told her you were lying down in the bathroom. She didn't believe me, so she sent Sally up to check, and you weren't there. She wants to see you tomorrow." All of a sudden, her face got hard, as if she were about to throw a rock at me. "Maybe you oughta try to sober up by then," she said and jumped out of the car.

I peeled away from the curb fast. Everybody can go take a flying leap, I thought as I raced through the afternoon traffic. Everybody! I don't need all this hassle. Big deal, one day out of the whole year I get drunk in school, big deal!

Chapter VII

I took a few extra pains sneaking into the house, but I needn't have bothered. My father was closeted in the downstairs study, and my mother was out shopping. I went up to the bathroom and stood under an icy shower for fifteen minutes. I was still pretty high when I got out, but I sounded and acted sober. Drinking during the day seemed to affect me differently.

When my mother got home, I helped her put away the groceries. We had a desultory conversation about school and the art show opening we were supposed to go to that evening with the out-of-town guests. Joyce skated around the topic of the night before. Finally she said, "What time did you get to bed?"

"I don't know," I said honestly. "Sometime after my straight flush." I smiled at her, but she wasn't amused. My mother's sense of humor was one of Carl's fictions, though he'd said it so often he probably believed it himself by now.

"You've been having quite a few late nights recently," my mother continued. That's a cute way of putting it, I thought. "Why don't you stay home tonight? You know how these openings are—"

"Fine," I interrupted. I didn't need convincing. I was exhausted, and inventing critical comments to impress strangers wasn't my idea of a relaxing outing. Besides, there was a baseball game on TV. "I'm going up to study," I informed her. "There's a TV dinner," she said. "And a fruit salad."

They left almost immediately, my father complaining that I wasn't coming. I'd taken a couple of nips from the bottle in my bedroom closet, but it was much nicer to make myself a gin and tonic and sip it in the living room. The last thing I wanted was to sober up. Then I'd have to think about Martha leaping out of the car as if she were a pit bull after prey, or my mother's weird indirect comments. Not to mention the upcoming discussion with Scotty, who seemed determined to hassle me to within an inch of a nervous breakdown. I shook my head. For someone who's doing pretty damn well, I thought, you've sure got a lot of people camped on your neck.

When I woke up the next morning, everything about the day before was hazy. Had I really taken the chemistry test? Or drunk with Sam in the vacant lot? I remembered Joyce's remark and thinking about Scotty, but not much beyond that. How could I black out on a couple of drinks? It didn't make sense.

The other surprise was my awful hangover, considering I must have crawled off to bed and passed out before eight. My head felt as though a group of grape stompers had used it for practice. I seriously thought about not going to school. But Joyce might be suspicious, and I'd promised to take the paper to the printer today. I had to go.

I pinched myself awake through English, and when I got to chemistry, our graded tests were already on our desks. I got a 94, which I could hardly believe. The questions looked incomprehensible. But I must have taken the exam. It was my writing.

My brain kept slipping off somewhere, and a couple of times I caught myself grabbing on to the edge of the desk as if that was going to make me come back. I shuffled from class to class until I got a note in math to go to gym during my lunch period. I didn't care anymore about Scotty seeing me with a hangover. I knew this one wasn't going away. All I wanted to do was get through the day and collapse on the other side somewhere.

I went right to the gym. Scotty was in her office, chain-smoking as usual. She motioned me in and then got up and shut the door. Serious. I was immediately claustrophobic. "I hope you're not feeling defensive today," she said.

I dropped my head in my hands. "Look," I said, "I'm not up to any long conversation. I can't take it. I got drunk yesterday, that's why I wasn't at practice. I'm hung over today. If you're throwing me off the team, do it, but don't hassle me about it."

"Thanks for telling me the truth. I'll return the favor. I don't want to throw you off the team. We need you, but not like this." She paused, and I was surprised at the little flicker of hope that sparked up in my chest. Who's this? I asked. I don't even know what's happening, and someone in there wants something? I shook my head. Scotty was talking again. "I'm worried, and so are other people. I want you on the team, Niki, but I want you to go to A.A. or some other alcoholic rehabilitation program. I think you're an alcoholic."

I blinked. "What?"

"I said I think—"

"I heard you. You don't have to say it again. The basis of my staying on the team is I go to A.A.? I want to get it straight, you know."

Scotty bit her lip. "Niki, why can't you—"

"Is that right?" I insisted.

"Yes." She looked me straight in the eyes and I looked her back.

"Well, forget it!" I shouted. "Take your lousy team and shove it. Nobody tells me what I should and shouldn't do! And nobody pities me! You get it?" I was out of my chair and I had raised my hand to clutch her by the shirt, but I caught myself in time.

She looked at me leaning halfway across her desk. "I didn't say anything about pity. Pity isn't the issue here at all. Alcoholism is a disease, a physical allergy like diabetes."

"I don't want to hear about it! It's no wonder I think I'm going crazy! Every fucking person around me has gone nuts! I think I'm the only sane one left. I want you to LEAVE ME ALONE!" My voice was shaking so much I could hardly breathe.

She turned away and stared out the window. "All right," she said. "I'll transfer you to Mrs. Michaels' P.E. class. You don't have to go today. I'll talk to her about it this afternoon. You can keep the same locker. I think that's about all." She kept staring out the window, her back to me.

A sob caught in my throat, and I wanted her to hold me, to help me, to make things all right. I stuck my fist between my teeth, opened the door, and ran outside. I kept running. Across the playing field, through the break in the fence, along the street, the tears flying off with the wind, running until I fell on somebody's front lawn. I rolled back and forth, moaning, sobs tearing up in my chest. I couldn't fight them any longer. I couldn't do anything. Oh, God, somebody help me! But there wasn't anybody there, and when I could breathe again, I got up and walked away.

Chapter VIII

I didn't drink that night. I went home, shut myself in my room, and started studying frantically. I had an English paper due Friday; for the first time in my life I started on an assignment earlier than the night before. Around seven-thirty I listened for the phone. By nine I knew Martha wasn't going to call. I wrote more. I was so miserable I turned out an excellent paper on grief, probably the best essay I'd written all year. I wondered what Martha was doing. And what had Scotty told the team? "Well, I gave her a choice, girls, and she took the easy way out." Easy, hah. I started to type up my paper.

I woke up clear-headed the next morning, ate a good breakfast, and actually smiled at people as I drove to school. I felt good. God, in comparison with yesterday I felt like an Olympic long-distance runner. I turned in my paper ahead of time to Mrs. Crandall, and she couldn't believe it. After chemistry I ran down to the journalism office and apologized to Mitch for not taking the paper to the printer.

"Oh, that's O.K., Niki," he said. "Bruce brought it down. You got a big game today, I hear."

"Yeah," I said. "With Washington. They almost beat us last time."

"O.K. Have your story in at the usual time. And I want you to write the editorial next issue. Start thinking about it, eh?"

I was thinking so hard when I went out that I had to sprint to math. I'd been so involved with softball that I'd forgotten Mitch would choose an editor soon for next year. If he gave me the editorial to write . . . I considered the other page editors. Page one and sports were seniors. Bruce was feature page editor, and I was editorial page editor. There was Richie in the darkroom, a super journalism freak, but he hadn't gotten into the nitty-gritty of layout and paste-up, so it was really between Bruce and me. I wondered why I hadn't realized all this earlier, so I could have been politicking, or at least driving the stupid paper to the printer instead of leaving it up to Bruce. Not smart. Well, I'd write a super editorial and put a lot of leadership into my page. I'd been sloughing off in journalism lately, not riding people enough. At least half the class took the course because it was easy, like art or yearbook. And you got a press card, so you could get in all the games free. The editor had to be able to extract some work out of all the free riders. I'd better write a good story today too. Damn. The game. I didn't want to cover the game. I'd rather never see any of our games. What had Scotty told everybody?

Then I got a summons to see Mr. Mansfield, my counselor. My optimism vanished in a flash. Had Scotty told him her cute theory?

But when I walked in his office, he was smiling broadly. "Well, there you are!" he crowed. "The SAT's just came in, and I wanted to congratulate you."

"Oh?" I said uncertainly. The Manse made me uncomfortable. He was always so hearty.

"Yup! You got the highest combined scores in the school. Not the highest individual, mind, but the highest combined." He gave me a computer printout, and I looked at my scores— 723 in English and 697 in math. "Any combined over 1200 is excellent," he said, "and you got over 1400. With your grades and these scores, you've got your pick of colleges."

He sat back and beamed at me, and I stumbled around for something to say. "Well," he prompted, "where are you thinking of going?"

"Uh, I guess the university. Private schools are too expensive. I thought I might take a couple of classes up there next year. You know how people do?" Pam, our present editor, only came to school for journalism and P.E. That sounded good to me, even if I'd just thought of it a second earlier.

His face fell. "Niki, you should have told me earlier. I'm almost sure it's too late." He bounced up and started going through papers scattered all around his bookshelves. I sat in suspense. "Nope!" he said triumphantly. "This Friday's the deadline. Here, fill this out now, and I'll get your transcripts Xeroxed, write a letter of recommendation, and we'll mail it off."

He disappeared, and I looked at the application. Why not? I started trying to match dates and events. Who knew when they'd graduated from sixth grade? I had to count backwards on my fingers. Martha would be going to the university. We could meet for lunch at one of those little cafes.... Of course Chuck and his dumb fraternity friends were also there. I didn't want to think about him. Let's see. Had I won any awards? I thought back. No, not that I could remember. Except Martha might not be speaking to me after the softball debacle, so maybe she wouldn't want to have lunch together....
I finished the application. Lunch and journalism were over, and I went straight to P.E.

Mrs. Michaels looked me over when I trotted up to her. "You're late," she said.

"I was in the counselor's office filling out forms."

"All right. We're playing softball. I don't want you pitching.

It wouldn't be fair for anyone else. So you can play shortstop or right field."

"Shortstop," I said. I started playing, but it was hard to keep my mind on the game. I kept watching the team work out on the other side of the field. I could tell Alice was having trouble. When we went into the dugout, I asked a distraught Mrs. Michaels if I could talk to Alice for a minute. She pinched her nose as if she were trying to quell the beginnings of a migraine. "Go ahead. We have thirty girls here. They all have to play." I ran across the field to where Alice and Sarah were warming up.

"Oh, good," Alice said. "Are you going to pitch?"

"No, I just thought I'd give you a few pointers."

"Oh, Niki, why don't you pitch? I'm not good enough, especially with Washington. Are you really that busy?"

I threw Sarah the ball. Scotty must have told the team I'd quit because I had too much to do. That was considerate. "Yeah, I really am too busy," I said. "I just spent all day applying to take courses at the university next year."

Alice smiled. "That's nice. But couldn't you pitch today? I need some time to get used to it."

"No," I said. "Now look. Take a few more chances. Don't worry about walking a couple of people. The batters will start swinging at bad pitches, wanting to get some action. Then you fire in a strike or two, and the batter's out."

"O.K.," Alice said dubiously.

I had her stand next to me, and we went through a series of deliveries. I was furious at myself for not helping her sooner, instead of right before an important game. What was the matter with me? But then I realized that both Alice and I had been assuming she wouldn't be pitching much until she was a senior. Now she was suddenly thrown into the starting pitcher slot as a sophomore. No wonder she was upset. She was wild at first, but she settled down, and I could see she would turn into an excellent pitcher if she didn't lose her nerve. It would have been much better to ease her in next year, each of us pitching half the games. But forget that. I stood in back of Sarah, acting as umpire while Alice completed her warm-ups. "Too high, Alice. Get it down. That's right. There you go." I laughed. "Not that far down. Alice, look. Whenever you throw it in the dirt, you overcompensate by pitching a high, easy one to get the range back. Only trouble is, they're going to smash those all over the field. You've gotta take more chances."

"O.K., Niki," Alice said. She started pitching wild again.

I looked behind me and saw that the Washington bus had pulled up. Alice was really freaked. "That's enough, Alice," I said. "You don't want to tire yourself out." She nodded gratefully and went into the dugout to put on her jacket. Sarah immediately jumped up to face me, and there was a new hostility in her eyes. "How come you're so busy all of a sudden?"

"I've been tired lately," I hedged.

Scotty trotted across the grass. "Niki, thanks for helping Alice."

"Sure. I wish I'd done it sooner."

Scotty shrugged. "None of us thought it was necessary till next year." Sarah glared at me while I nodded.

"I've got to get my notebook," I said, edging toward the gym. "I have to write up the game for the paper."

Sarah's face flushed even more, and I turned away quickly. She was thinking, If she's going to be here anyway, why can't she pitch? I felt like a fool. Maybe it would have been better if Scotty had told the truth. No. That was stupid.

I sprinted back to the gym, grabbed my notebook and a pen, and settled myself in the bleachers away from the other spectators. I realized it was going to be tricky writing this story. What was I going to say about myself? I figured I'd stick in a sentence at the end: Niki Etchen has quit the team because of pressing obligations, or something like that. Or maybe not mention it at all. But if Frank quit the boys' team, there'd be interviews and general freak-outs.

Alice didn't do badly the first inning, though I was on the mound every second in my head. It was terrible, because I was really psyched up to pitch. What if I lied to Scotty, told her I was going to A.A.? No, that was blown. Why should I have to lie in order to pitch? I started hating Scotty. She must feel like a real dope. Here I am, healthy as a lion, and she's keeping me out. You quit, I reminded myself. But what choice did I have? She drove me into a corner.

Alice fell apart with three women on in the fourth, and Scotty put Teri in. Teri walked the first, bringing in another run, and then managed to pull out of the inning with a force play at home. Teri was a natural athlete, so she *could* pitch, but she wasn't a good pitcher. Sarah kept glancing at me from the backstop, and I wrote meaningless phrases in my notebook. The score was 9–4. There was no way we could win. Teri tried hard, but Washington's hitters were too good. I thought about what Alice must be going through. Teri was a senior, and there were no other sophomores or juniors who could pitch. It was all on Alice, and she'd blown up under pressure. The game ended 14–6. Everyone but Martha ran off to the showers. She came over to me. I occupied myself by staring at my feet until she cleared her throat.

"Niki? Would you drive me home?"

"Sure," I said gratefully. "I'll be out here."

Martha glanced at a few of the Washington players, who were moving toward us, egging each other on with catcalls about our team. "I think you better come in the gym."

I stood up, closing the notebook, and we started walking. "Hey, punk!" someone yelled. "Break your arm?" Laughter.

Martha and I continued on, until the voice was right behind us.

"Hey, girl. I asked you a question." I felt fingers digging into my shoulder, and I spun around to face three grinning Washington players. "Didja break your arm?"

"Let go," I said.

"What'd you say to me, girl?"

"I said, Let go!" The pain of her grip must have showed in my face. Martha shot her arm up to try to break the hold. And they were on us, all three of them. Somebody's fist connected with my nose; blood sprayed across my shirt. I heard Martha cry out, and I saw her down in the dirt, her arm yanked up behind her neck. I kicked the one on Martha in the face, and somebody retaliated by kicking me in the stomach. I doubled over in pain, and my head was pressed into the dust. I couldn't breathe. I started to panic. Blood was flooding out of my nose, and I was choking from the pain in my gut.

Then the pressure eased suddenly. I looked up in time to see Martha crouching over me, holding a girl by the shoulders. Another foot shot out, Martha went down, and the girl she had been holding spun after her. I grabbed her and threw her off. Washington's coach ran in like a whirlwind, yanked me by the arm, and flung me a few feet away. I landed hard, and it took me a moment to catch my breath.

Martha was screaming, "Are you crazy? They attacked us!"

"Never mind, girls," the coach said, shepherding away her charges. "I'm filing a complaint against these two, and against this team. Come on."

"You're insane!" Martha started running after them, but I managed to get up and catch her.

"Martha, wait! She's saying that to save face or something. She's not going to do anything. Come on."

I pulled her away, and Martha hung on to me. "Wait, Niki, my leg." I felt her sinking, so I let her down gradually. "One of those creeps kicked me. It hurts like hell." I pulled off her shoe, and she tried to wiggle her leg. "Oh, God!" Tears started dripping down her face. She wiped them away angrily. "First we blow the game, and then this. Damn, it hurts!"

I threw back my head and sniffed hard, trying to stop my nose from bleeding. "Stand up and lean on me, Martha. We'll get back to the gym, and Scotty can put some ice on it."

We hobbled across the field, Martha leaning on me hard. I wasn't sure I could get her all the way back myself. Then I saw Teri come out the gym door. "Teri!" I shouted. She looked around, up at the school. "Teri!"

She finally saw us and ran across the field. "Jesus Christ, what happened!" She grabbed on to me, because I looked worse probably, all covered with blood.

But I motioned to Martha. "Help me get her into the gym," I said. "Her leg is messed up." I was beginning to feel faint, but Teri was fresh from the shower, and we made it to the gym quickly. Scotty had been alerted.

She motioned to Teri. "You take Niki over there. Get the bleeding stopped. I'll handle Martha."

A moment later I was lying on a bench, my head back, Teri putting cold cloths on my nose and lips. Sarah was washing off my arms and hands with warm water. "Boy," she said, "they sure stomped you. What happened to your hand?"

I wiggled my fingers. They were all moving. "I don't know. Stepped on it with cleats, I guess." My face felt like the whole Washington team had trekked across it on the way to their bus.

"I think your nose is broken," Teri said. "Can you breathe through it?"

I tried. "Yeah, it's O.K., but it hurts like crazy."

I stood up, and Teri swabbed my face off with the warm cloth. "You look a little better," she said.

"Thanks, Teri. I want to go see about Martha."

"They're in the little room off the gym."

I went back and knocked on the door. "Who is it?" Scotty asked.

"Niki," I answered.

"Come on in." I shut the door behind me. Martha lay on the table, the muscles in her leg in knots. She'd been vomiting with the pain, and her eyes were filmed over. Scotty was massaging her leg. "Niki, go get a towel and a mop and clean this up."

I moved quickly, frightened, and after I'd cleaned up, I got a sponge and wiped off Martha's face. She looked at me for a minute; I could see the pain pulsating deep in her eyes. "Martha, are you O.K.?"

"I guess so," she mumbled. "It hurts so much."

"What's the matter?" I asked Scotty.

"Some ligaments are torn, but then her leg went into cramps. That's what's hurting her most now. What happened?"

"Some of the people on the Washington team jumped us."

"Their coach blamed it on us," Martha said through clenched teeth. "She said she was going to file a complaint. There were three of them at first and then more. One of them kicked Niki and held her down with her face in the dirt. She was trying to kill her!"

"Who started it?" Scotty asked.

"They did," we both said together. "They were hassling me about why I wasn't pitching," I explained.

Scotty didn't say anything. Her massaging was paying off. Martha's muscles were relaxing and her face eased. I sponged her off again. "I just wish we hadn't lost the game too," Martha said.

I felt weird. Here I was in the locker room, as though I'd played. Scotty might see, after this fight and listening to Martha, how much being on the team meant to me. "Scotty?" I said.

Scotty looked up at me. "Any time you do what I suggested, you can start pitching again," she said. "That's it."

Martha looked confused. "But I thought you'd quit," she said to me. Silence. Scotty's face was set hard as cement.

Finally I said, "I'll tell you about it on the way home."

Scotty nodded at me. "I told everyone you'd quit," she said. "You can say whatever you want. You're driving Martha home?"

I nodded.

"All right, I'll have Teri help you bring her to the car. When you get home, put her on the bed with her leg slightly raised. Don't come to school tomorrow or Friday, Martha, and move around as little as possible. Get her a cane or something to support her, Niki. If you feel up to it, you can come on Monday. If not, give me a call. I'll clear tomorrow and Friday with the office. And, Niki, if you find you can't breathe through one of your nostrils, go to the hospital right away. They'll open it up. Your nose is broken."

"I know," I said. It was throbbing, horribly painful.

"Oh, Niki!" Martha said. "And your mouth is all cut up."

"I'm O.K.," I said. "Come on, let's get you home to bed."

We helped her off the table, and Scotty called Teri in. But at the door Martha hesitated. "Scotty, this means I won't be able to play, doesn't it?"

Scotty nodded. "That's right. I'm afraid it does." She walked away, and I felt as though someone had stuck a sword through my chest. Christ, her championship team is falling apart at the climax of the season, and the allocation will be decided soon. If we start losing . . .

You're not on the team anymore, I reminded myself. But damn! She loses her pitcher and first baseman and one of her best hitters . . . I started helping Martha to the car.

Chapter IX

On the way to Martha's we had instant replay of the fight about fifteen times. Talking drove the shock back and distracted Martha from wondering why I'd left the team. When we got to her house, I unlocked the door and half-carried her up the steps. It made me feel good to help her, as if I'd actually found something I could do.

I propped her up on the bed and told her about my SAT scores and applying for university classes next year. Her face lit up, and I got embarrassed. I was so pleased I had to rush downstairs to get her some water. I'd been worried she would tell me to cram it after the double blow of my drinking in the vacant lot and then leaving the team.

When I came back upstairs, she said, "What's this you're supposed to do if you want to pitch?"

"Oh, Scotty has one of her dippy ideas." I handed her the glass, and she drank thirstily.

"Better," she sighed. "What is it? Or would you rather not tell me? You don't have to, you know."

I didn't want to tell her, but if I clammed up, she'd decide it was too close to home. All I could do was scoff at it. "Oh, she asked me to go to A.A. or some alcoholic rehabilitation program." I stumbled over the word "alcoholic." It sounded horrible.

"She thinks you're an alcoholic?" Martha said it right out, no stumbling.

"That's what she said, but I guess she wants me to go a couple of times as an educational experience, sort of."

Martha nodded. "That seems reasonable. Why not?"

By making Scotty's ultimatum sound so harmless, I'd backed myself into a corner. "Look, Martha, it's not like going down for a blood test to see if you have V.D. When you're an alcoholic, you're an alcoholic. It doesn't go away with a shot of penicillin."

"But don't you want to know?"

I blew up. "What's wrong with you, anyway? Of course I'm not an alcoholic. Am I lying on Skid Row begging for dimes? Good God, I just got the highest combined score on the SAT's. Does that sound like an alcoholic?"

"Stop yelling," Martha said. "You're going to start your nose bleeding again. Skid Row and the SAT's don't have anything to do with it. My uncle is an alcoholic. Well, he goes to A.A., and he hasn't drunk in years, but he was always smart and had a good job even when he was drinking."

"He might not have been one then," I insisted. "Maybe he stopped drinking for nothing." I shivered. The thought of not drinking for years sent chills through me.

"God, Niki! It's not so horrible! My parents hardly ever drink. On Christmas they have some sherry or something. You think everyone drinks twenty-four hours a day and that's normal."

"I do not," I said. "Look, I'm going downtown for half an hour. I'll be back."

"All right. Take my house key. That way I won't have to let you back in. Kenny has his own key."

I almost crawled down the stairs, I was so sore; but once I

got in the car, I turned the radio up really loud. I couldn't understand Martha's reaction. She didn't have any conception of what a big deal it would be to be an alcoholic. She acted as if it was an everyday occurrence like ingrown toenails or something. In one way, it was a nice reaction. At least she knew alcoholics weren't weak-willed or evil, and she didn't act as if they were all mental cases. But nonetheless, it was a huge deal . . . I forced myself to stop thinking and went in search of a cane.

I found the perfect cane at the Salvation Army. It was black enameled, with little silver-colored stars and a fancy silver handle. Very posh. When I bought it, the clerk stared at me oddly. In fact, every person on the street seemed to be compelled to give me a second glance when I walked by. I patted my clothes self-consciously. No, all together. Driving back, I accidentally touched my nose and yelped with the pain. But if I kept my hands away, I forgot about it. My whole face had numbed out.

When I walked in the bedroom with the cane, Martha burst out laughing. "Niki, that's lovely. You make quite a picture. Go look at yourself. And give me the cane. It's beautiful."

I went into the bathroom and stared at the creature in the mirror. Both my eyes were blackened, my nose was swollen and tilted off to one side, and my lips were puffy and cut up. It looked as if someone had slammed me repeatedly in the face with a sledgehammer. Apart from all the bruises, I seemed different, as if a subtle hand had rearranged my features while I wasn't looking. Must be the nose.

I walked back into the bedroom. "Charming," I said. "No wonder everybody was staring at me."

"No kidding. Come 'ere." I sat at the side of the bed while Martha examined my face. She had a gleam in her eye. "Niki," she said. "Suppose I just carefully pushed your nose over."

74

"No!" I shouted. "You can't imagine how sore it is. I can't touch it, not even the skin."

She reached out tentatively. "It only has to go to the left maybe a quarter of an inch. But I guess it might hurt."

"Hurt is not the word, Martha. Scream and faint would be more like it. Or murder."

"Murder? You or me?"

I tried to laugh, but my face felt heavy as a bag of wet sand. "You for sure, me probably."

"All right, but it's crooked, and now is the time to change it."

"Never mind. It'll give me a rakish look, like those guys with the scarred cheeks in Germany."

"O.K. Don't get angry now, but I had Kenny go to the library while you were gone, and I want you to listen to what this book says." I sat stunned as she started to read the part about blackouts in *Alcohol Dependence*.

"Hold it," I said. "I've already read that."

"Oh. Well, did you know it's a disease similar to diabetes and might be related to blood sugar levels? See, it says here most alcoholics don't like sweet things, which is you for sure. You're the only person I know that acts as if it's torture to eat an ice cream cone. And this business about the personality change. You're like Dr. Jekyll and Mr. Hyde. And one out of ten people—"

"Martha. Martha. Please. Look." All of a sudden, tears welled up in my eyes, and I was shocked, because I was only going to tell her to shut up. "Martha, please don't do this. You don't care, see, but it's a big thing to me. You're treating me as if I'm your current pet project. First you want to change my nose, and now you want to convince me I'm an alcoholic."

Martha closed the book and shut her eyes for a second. "God, I'm such a moron," she said. "I'm sorry, Niki. I'll keep my mouth shut. I'm worried, but it's not fair to lay it on you."

"O.K.," I said, glad that she'd seen what I meant right away. "Let's forget it. How about if I read to you? There's a couple of new magazines downstairs."

"Don't your lips hurt?"

When she said it, I realized my whole face was throbbing. The numbness was wearing off. "You're right. Scrabble?"

Her parents came home in the middle of the game, which was lucky for me, since I always lost to Martha. They exclaimed over my face and Martha's leg, and it occurred to me I was going to have to encounter my parents sometime.

I tried to sneak in the house, but I wasn't very successful. Carl boomed out, "Who won?"

"They did," I said, but by this time I could hardly talk. My lips were too swollen.

"What?" He walked into the hall. "Niki!"

"What's the matter?" Joyce came rushing from the kitchen. Oh no, I thought. "Niki! Your nose! And your mouth! Your eyes!"

"It's no big deal," I said.

"Have you lost your mind?" Joyce shouted. "We have to go down to the hospital right away."

"Absolutely not," I said.

"What happened?" Carl put in.

"A fight. With some of the Washington kids."

"Your nose is broken. We have to get it straightened."

"I am not going to the hospital. That's final."

"You can't go through life with a crooked nose!" Joyce wailed.

"Niki, you're a beautiful girl. We could go down there. It wouldn't take long—"

"No!" I shouted. "I'm going to take a bath, and that's it!"

"Oh, this stupid softball!" Joyce rounded on my father. "Carl, it's all your fault! She's seventeen! She should be going to proms, not—"

"I quit the team," I said.

"What?" my father thundered. "You get beat up a little, and you quit—"

"A little? I'm glad you're finally showing some sense, Niki."

"I quit before the fight," I explained. "I didn't play today. The fight started—"

"Why did you quit?" Carl shouted.

"Can't you see?" Joyce yelled. "Does she have to come home in an ambulance?"

"Because I'm too busy," I said lamely.

"What kind of excuse is that?"

"A good excuse! And now we're going to the hospital and have your nose straightened."

"Why won't anybody listen to me?" I yelled. "I am not going to the hospital. I quit the team. I applied to go to the university next year. I got my SAT's back. I got the highest combined score in the school. I'll almost surely be accepted. And that's it. That is absolutely it!" I turned away and started walking to the bathroom.

"What does next year have to do with this year?" Carl called down the hall. I didn't answer. I locked the bathroom door and ran the water hard.

Chapter X

I didn't drink for a week. It was kind of hard rationalizing not drinking, but I figured I'd cool out for a while. Other people didn't drink all the time. There wasn't some hard and fast rule written across the horizon that said you sat down at six and started boozing. Or so Martha claimed anyway. I wasn't sure I believed her, but since it fit in with what I wanted to do, I decided to give her the benefit of the doubt. After all, drinking when you felt like it seemed the sensible thing to do, and wasn't my father always praising me for being sensible?

Actually he wasn't praising me for much of anything at the moment. It was hard hanging out with them when I wasn't drinking, so I stuck to my room, telling them I had a bunch of long papers to write. But we had to see each other at breakfast, and Carl couldn't let one day go by without a reference to my quitting the team. "What if McCovey decided he was too damned busy to make it out to the park one day? Hunh? Or Frank. Isn't he that friend of yours that's getting the scholarships? He manages to drag himself to the games even though he has to negotiate offers and be a senior in high school at the same time."

It was no use explaining to Carl that junior year was by far the busiest, that seniors were marking time until college or career. The explanations were especially dumb, since being busy wasn't the reason I'd quit. I would stare at him across the breakfast table and say, "I don't want to discuss it." Then he would blow up, and I would dash off to school, and the next morning we'd do it all over again.

I made up for everything by throwing myself into journalism. Suddenly I became the editorial wonder. Nobody did anything good enough, so I did everything over. And I worked hard on my editorial, rewriting it again and again until everything was the way I wanted it.

Martha came back to school on Tuesday, and she was instantly bored to death. "Being a senior is such a drag anyway," she said during class break. "Especially after Christmas. The colleges don't care, everybody's going to graduate, there's no reason to be here at all. Now that I can't play ball—"

"Start a new art project," I advised. "Something big enough to carry you through the next two weeks. And not," I added quickly, "my nose."

"You look a lot better," she said. "Your eyes and your mouth anyway."

"Thanks heaps," I said.

The big sophomore kid from journalism ran by and said over his shoulder, "Mitch wants to see you right away."

"This is it!" I said to Martha. "He's going to pick the editor!"

"O.K., don't bust a gut. Go on down there."

"Meet you at the car after school," I said. I ran down the steps, pushing past knots of kids on the first lunch shift. I made myself slow down when I got to the journalism corridor. It wouldn't do to go storming in.

I pushed open the door and confronted a troubled-looking

Mitch. "I wanted to tell you," he said, "before I told the class. I picked Bruce for editor next year."

My face fell a mile. He sighed. "It's funny, I had you as first choice for a long time. But since I asked you to write the editorial, you've been a real bear around here. Riding everyone. Hold on"—he raised his hand as I started to speak—"I know you were trying to impress me. But the thing is, you're an intense person, Niki. When you were on the ball team, it was O.K.; your attention was divided. But if you were editor, and without the team, I think nothing anyone did would suit you. You'd end up redoing the whole paper. Nobody's going to learn anything that way. I decided Bruce would be a better leader."

"Oh," I said.

"But I want you to stay on the staff. I was wondering if you'd like to do sports next year? With, um, full control." He winked, and I grinned a little in spite of my disappointment. It was a sop, but it was a good one. No woman had ever edited the sports page, and he was essentially giving me free rein. I wouldn't have to work under Bruce.

I thought about it. The sports page was the most widely read, and the photographic possibilities were enormous. Which reminded me. I thought I might throw a little extra into the bargaining process. "How 'bout if I work in the darkroom next year too, Mitch?"

He scowled. He never liked more than two photographers, and he had his all picked. "All right," he said, "you win. Sports and photography." We shook hands on it. I'd lost and he'd lost, but we'd both come out ahead. I felt pretty good when I split.

"My ego's a little pricked," I explained to Martha. "But it'll be fun editing the sports page."

Martha fiddled around with the car door handle. "I can see what he means, Niki. You are awfully intense. Unbearable might be a better word."

"Look, Martha," I snapped, "how come you're always on everybody else's side? I'm supposed to be your best friend."

Martha refused to be ruffled. "As you are, kiddo, as you are. But your ego could stand a little pricking."

"I don't think so," I said, putting the car in gear. "Everything lately has been a blow. First the team and now the paper. I've lost a lot."

I started to feel sorry for myself, but Martha hit me over the head with her notebook. "Home, James. Or actually, try the ice cream store."

"All right." While she got her cone, I went across the street and used my fake ID to buy a six-pack of beer. I figured I deserved a beer or two. It had been a heavy day. We drove out to the park and threw a ball around. It wasn't much fun for Martha probably, since she couldn't move more than two steps in any direction, but she threw me a lot of flies and grounders, and I got a good workout.

"Do they have a women's team up at the university?" I asked after she'd begged off.

"You know, I don't have any idea. It never occurred to me to ask. I guess I figured I'd be too busy. But it'd sure be nice."

"Sure would," I said. I was into my third beer and feeling mellow. "Maybe I could take P.E. up there next year. Frances did that. She's taking bowling or something so she doesn't have to take high school P.E."

"That way you could pitch," Martha said. "Only you probably couldn't play on the team until you were an actual full-time student."

"You're probably right. Guess I'll have to spend my time studying next year. God, what a drag!"

"You *could* pitch if you wanted to," Martha pointed out.

"Forget that idea. At least up at the university they won't be infected by Scotty's disease."

"Which is?"

"Hate-Niki-itis," I growled.

"Oh, Niki. Hey, give me one of those beers. She did what she thought was right, that's all."

"Yeah, but if she hadn't thrown me off the team, I'd have gotten the editor's job. Mitch as much as said so."

"You were the one who was pushy and demanding. How you act isn't Scotty's fault. It's not as if she went around spreading rumors about you."

"How do I know?" I said. "She probably did. Maybe she told Mitch I was irresponsible or a maniac. Or even paid him off so he'd give Bruce the job."

"Paranoia," Martha trilled. "You sound like a psychotic on a lousy TV show."

"Gee thanks, Martha," I flared. "First I'm an alcoholic. Now I'm psychotic. And we all know I'm neurotic. That leaves me in a fine mess, hunh?"

Martha sipped her beer and put the can at her side. She lay on her back and shielded her eyes from the sun. I realized I was being a fool. "You sure have gotten sensitive lately," she said. "It's hard to talk to you sometimes."

"I feel awful," I said defensively. "My life is falling apart. It's either way up or way down. All the stuff that's happened in the last month has been either horrible or wonderful. There's nothing in between. It's a good thing there's booze. Otherwise I'd go insane."

"You think drinking keeps you sane?"

"Sure. Whenever the pressure builds up, I get drunk. Then I'm O.K. again for a while. It's like lifting the lid on a steam cooker."

"I suppose I can see that," Martha said. "It's getting late. Let's split, eh?"

When I got back to the house, I joined my parents for cocktails and dinner. Joyce was obviously pleased. She kept making suggestions about shopping trips and refurbishing my wardrobe and had I heard any news about Chuck? I think she figured I'd quit the team so I could get on with my real lifework of being belle of the ball.

Carl grumped in his easy chair, but my mother and I ignored him. Finally, over dinner, he said, "What's done is done. Let's talk about the university."

Even though I was having fun with them, I was glad when they went to bed, because I wanted a gin and tonic. They had all these ideas about when you could drink certain kinds of drinks. More rules, I thought. My parents' rules, Scotty's rules. . . . She was messing up my life, and worse, she was getting away with it. The business with Mitch was her fault, no matter what Martha said. I never would have been so gung-ho in journalism if I hadn't been thrown off the team.

I heard my parents close the door to their bedroom, and I eased open the latch of the liquor cabinet. They didn't like me drinking unless they were there, as if they were monitoring me. I fixed a mostly-gin gin and tonic and sipped at it while I glanced through *Time* magazine. But I kept smarting. I was supposed to go to A.A. when I was a perfectly successful pitcher, best in the league? Ridiculous. But she almost made it seem reasonable. And then Mitch essentially said I was too good to be editor, that I had to make everything right. The great stampede toward mediocrity. They were all trying to make me lose my self-confidence. That could be heavy for a kid of seventeen—not me, of course, but for some other kid. What I'd gone through in the last month could crush a person for life!

I gulped down the rest of my drink and checked the level of the gin bottle. A little more wouldn't hurt even though I was getting pretty plowed. Might as well go all the way. Who cared anyhow? Scotty sure didn't, even though she supposedly wanted me to talk to her. Why would I talk to her? It'd be like a condemned person wanting to have a heart-to-heart chat with his executioner. Here I was, good at two specific things, pitching and journalism, and Scotty was preventing me from doing either of them, because I wouldn't knuckle under or take second-best for good enough. I should call and tell her. I looked at the clock. Eleven-fifteen. Too late.

I stumbled over to the liquor cabinet and checked out the gin again. It was nearly to the halfway point, so I poured an inch of my father's bourbon in my glass. When I got back to my chair again, I remembered tomorrow was another game. Here I am, I thought, getting drunk instead of being in bed asleep, all because Scotty's decided to make wrecking my life her second career. What the hell does she have against me? I realized with a start she'd never even heard my side of the story. She sat there handing down her dictums as if she was Moses on the mountain. Maybe if I explained stuff to her, she'd see . . .

I decided to risk snatching a six-pack from the refrigerator. I could always buy one and put it back before my parents noticed. I shut the front door quietly and went out to my car. You have to drive carefully, I cautioned myself. I started down the street at fifteen miles an hour.

I heard myself saying something about Carmel, and then it slipped away. I was sitting up. Martha sat beside me, and we were in the back of a station wagon. "So what do you want to do?" Martha prompted. "About Carmel?"

I looked at her. What . . . ? Martha wasn't with me earlier, was she? No, I was sure she wasn't. And whose car was this? "Martha," I mumbled. "I'm sorry, but what are you doing here, wherever we are? And what car is this?"

"She's coming out of a blackout," a voice from the front seat said. I spun around and almost fell off the seat. Teri reached her arm out to steady me.

84

Martha lit a cigarette in the dark. "Is that true? You don't remember what we were talking about?"

I shook my head. Jesus, I was drunk. "I remember leaving my house. I was going to talk to Scotty. I was driving carefully. That's all I can remember."

Martha checked her watch. "As near as I can figure, that was three hours ago. It's two-thirty now."

"Oh," I said. I was hopelessly confused. I felt something in my hand. A beer. I gulped at it. "You've been holding that for an hour," Martha said. "I asked you if you wanted me to get rid of it for you, but you had such a fit I let you keep it."

"But what are you doing here? I wasn't with you or Teri. What happened?"

Silence. "It'd probably be better if you didn't know, Niki," Teri said. She sounded tired.

I panicked. "No, you have to tell me! I'll go insane if you don't tell me! What did I do?" My voice rose, and Martha took my hand.

"It's O.K. We'll tell you. Teri just thought you'd rather not know."

I knew it was going to be bad. "I've gotta have another beer," I said. "Is there any more? I had a six-pack—"

"That one you're holding is the last. And the stores are closed."

"Oh. We can go to my parents. I can fix you both a drink and—"

"Hey, Niki," Martha said, "it's two-thirty. Teri's parents aren't home. She asked if we wanted to stay there. I told my parents you were upset and we were both going to spend the night. And you said your parents wouldn't notice you were gone and would think you'd left early in the morning for school. At least that's what you said when you were blacked out."

I thought about it. It was probably true. I was glad to see I was so bright when I was unconscious. "Yeah, that's O.K.," I said. "But do you have any beer or anything at your house?" Teri started the car. "There's a few cans in the fridge." Relief. "I don't think I could stand hearing this without a beer," I said to Martha. I smiled, to keep it light, but she looked grim and kept holding my hand. I realized I was scared. It freaked me out that Martha and Teri knew all this stuff that happened when I was blacked out, that they had power over my sanity. If only I had something to drink, then I'd feel better. It wouldn't be so bad. I started shaking.

Martha squeezed my hand harder. "We're almost there," she said.

We got out, and I began to stagger up the walk. "Lemme help you," Teri offered.

"No," I said proudly. "I've always made it on my own steam before. I'll do it again." I tried to walk straight, but my body wouldn't do it. I didn't have any balance. It was weird walking with them, me plunging off the sidewalk into the roses every two seconds. When Teri unlocked the door, I reeled into the house and started toward the kitchen.

"I'll get it," Teri said. "You stay here. Martha, you want anything?"

"A ginger ale if you have it."

"Right."

I slumped down in a chair, wondering how I could find out how many beers were left. I'd drink differently if there were two beers than if there were four. Two I'd sip, four I'd gulp.

Teri came back with the beer and two ginger ales. "There's three left after this one, Niki." I nodded gratefully. Teri explained to Martha: "My old man's an al— Well, he drinks. He always wants to know how many are left after the stores are closed." Martha nodded, watching me as I tore off the tab and drank thirstily.

Suddenly I didn't want to know what happened. The beer made it O.K. But I figured I had to ask, since I'd had such a fit about it before. "What did I do?"

"You drove over to Scotty's," Martha said. "She wasn't there. She was at a softball conference down south, not flying in till seven this morning. Her roommate explained all that to you, and you insisted Scotty was hiding in the house. You said she'd never leave the night before a game. You pushed the roommate aside and went raving around the house, trying to find Scotty. Laura, the roommate, phoned Scotty while you were looking in closets and under beds. Scotty told her to call the police."

"What a creep!" I said.

"My God, Niki, what do you expect. I mean—"

"Don't argue," Teri interrupted, "Just tell her."

"All right. Laura didn't want to do that. She teaches P.E. at State, and Scotty had told her about you. She didn't want you to get into more trouble, especially since you had obviously driven there. Scotty gave her my number. Laura called me, and I remembered Teri's parents had gone out of town and left the station wagon. That was lucky, since I never could have handled you myself."

Martha paused for breath. I was mesmerized, like a small child being told an interesting story. It didn't relate to me at all.

"We got there and dragged you off. You were fighting, but you were so drunk it wasn't too difficult. We got you in the car, and you started saying that Scotty would be sorry when she realized what she'd done. I thought you were just babbling, but all of sudden, you threw open the car door and jumped out. Luckily, Teri was braking for a stop sign, and you landed all right. You went running off. We stopped the car and chased you. Teri caught you as you threw yourself in front of a car. She yanked you away. The driver was furious—he wanted to call the police. We got rid of him, and I slapped you because you were hysterical. We dragged you back to the car, but we were afraid to move, since you kept threatening to jump out, and I can't run. Then you started talking about Carmel, about how your life was over at seventeen, you might as well kill yourself, but if you went to Carmel you might recover some lost spark and start over or something. . . . The rest you know."

I put down the beer. I hadn't tasted it since Martha got to the part about my jumping out of the car. It hadn't seemed like a fairy tale after that. I didn't know what to say.

"You want some milk, Niki?" Teri asked.

I nodded. Teri brought out a quart of milk and a glass and poured some out. When I finished that, she poured some more. "I'm sorry," I said halfway through the second glass. "I don't know what else to do but thank you both and apologize."

"You—" Martha started, but Teri cut her off.

"Hold on, Martha. We had a choice. No one forced us to go on a rescue mission. It doesn't obligate Niki to us, as if she has to pay us back or something."

Martha thought about that for a while and sighed. "You're right," she said. "Is anyone ready for bed? Tomorrow's a school day, and it's now past three A.M."

"I'm going to sit here awhile," I said dully. I felt like that car I'd thrown myself in front of had crushed me.

"Will you be all right?" Martha asked.

"Yeah. I need to be alone for a few minutes."

"O.K." She got up.

Teri said, "Second bedroom on the left. You can share a bed with Martha. It's big. . . . Niki, I hope you don't mind my asking this, but have you ever had DT's?"

"No!" I said, horrified.

"O.K. I wanted to know what to expect. See you in the morning."

Teri and Martha went upstairs, and I sat there shell-shocked, unable to think. I kept saying over and over, This is heavy, you can't trust yourself, you might kill yourself when you're blacked out and don't know what you're doing, you're going to have to watch yourself every minute from now on. I felt like two people, as if there was a raging beast inside me that had to be strictly controlled. I was scared. Then I don't remember any more, so I guess I passed out.

I woke about six, shivering, and I washed my mouth out and drank some water. My stomach was bad. I was shaky, and my mind was totally disoriented. It kept flipping here and there, and I couldn't direct it at all. I was horribly alone. I went upstairs and crawled into bed next to Martha. I wanted her to comfort me, but I was afraid to wake her up. I was sure she hated me. Finally I hurt so much I had to chance it. I touched her hand. She woke a little, smiled sleepily, and threw her arm across me. I felt as if I'd been saved. I moved closer and fell asleep.

When I woke again, Teri was standing in the open doorway sipping at a glass of milk. Martha's head was pressed against my shoulder, and I disengaged myself carefully so she wouldn't wake up. I followed Teri down to the kitchen.

"How do you feel?"

"Like somebody dropped an atom bomb on me. Nothing hurts especially, but I'm incredibly wasted."

Teri nodded and brought out some soda crackers. "Could you eat these?"

I shook my head. "God, Teri, what am I going to say to Scotty and this mythical roommate?"

"Nothing. It's already happened. They're going to think what they want to think, no help from you. Here, try a little milk." She gave me the glass, and I could hardly hold it. I raised it to my lips and swallowed twice. I felt it hit my stomach, cold as ice. We both waited. I sensed it warming. It was all right.

"Good," Teri said. "Drink milk as often as you can and try some crackers later."

"You seem to have a lot of practice doing this."

"Yeah, my father, he's in and out of A.A. He sobers up for a few months, and then he goes off the wagon again. I was glad they left. He's drinking now, and I got tired of hassling with him."

"So you hassle with me instead," I said.

"That's by choice. I figured Martha would need some help anyway. This is all new to her."

"Umm," I muttered noncommittally. "Oh, I passed out on your couch, and then I moved upstairs later. That's O.K., I hope."

"Sure. I came back down and sat with you awhile. I wanted to make sure you weren't going to start convulsing. You were shaking and gritting your teeth, but I figured it wasn't bad enough to go to the hospital for."

I shook my head to clear it. I thought I hadn't heard right. "What?"

"You didn't know you did that? I guess it's not DT's but some minor form or maybe pre-DT's or something. Your whole body starts trembling and you grit your teeth."

"I was doing this while I was asleep?"

"Unh-hunh."

I was staring at the linoleum, wondering why my body and my head were betraying me, when Martha walked in. She stretched. "Nice day. Can't you die from DT's?"

Teri nodded. "Yeah, you can, but that's mostly old people

who've drunk for years and are undernourished and weak. It's highly unlikely that Niki would die."

Martha stretched like a big comfortable cat. "I see we missed the call to the old brick schoolhouse."

"I set the alarm, but since Niki wouldn't make it, and we're both seniors, I figured we could shine it for a day."

They wandered around making breakfast. I couldn't believe they would discuss the possibility of my death from DT's that I didn't even know I had and then calmly switch to some other topic. A chill ran through me, and Teri got a blanket from the front room and draped it over my shoulders.

"What do you want, Niki?" Martha said, holding up a spatula. "Eighteen eggs and ten rashers of bacon?" She turned to Teri. "Niki always eats like a bear when she's hung over."

"Not today," Teri said. "I'll be surprised if she can eat any more than a cracker before six."

"Really?" Martha looked at me. "Niki, what's the matter? You look upset."

"I am. I can't think. My mind keeps jumping back and forth, and you two are so calm! I mean, I never knew I did that, that . . . shaking. I'm scared!" My voice broke, and tears started dropping down my face. I was appalled. I couldn't seem to keep it together.

Martha put down the spatula, and I saw her eyes fill up with tears too. "But Niki, you won't get help. I mean, what are we supposed to do? If you'd go to A.A.—"

"Martha," Teri warned.

"What is all this?" I asked. "What's this little byplay between the two of you?"

Martha sighed and sat down next to me. "Teri's been going to these groups for friends of alcoholics. She's been telling me all this stuff. Like the drinker has to want to stop for herself. It makes it worse to try to push her into stopping. And I can't help you want to stop. It has to be your decision. And not to talk about it unless you want to, and I can't protect you from what you do when you're drunk. Stuff like that."

I swallowed. "Oh," I said. "But getting drunk doesn't make me an alcoholic."

"If you're not an alcoholic, Niki, I don't know who is."

Teri laughed. "You can recite it, Martha, but you haven't heard a word I've said. Niki, do you think you could eat a piece of bacon?"

"No," I said, shuddering. "And even if I am . . . one, that doesn't mean I want to stop drinking."

"That's right," Teri said cheerfully.

"My God, Teri—"

"Martha, honestly, there's no way you can make her want to stop. She has to want it for herself. So forget it."

"Hm-m-m," Martha said. She scooped bacon and eggs on two plates. "Are you sure you don't want anything?"

"No. I mean, yes, I'm sure. I'm going upstairs. O.K.?"

Teri nodded, and the two of them sat down to eat. I climbed the stairs slowly and got back into bed. I couldn't believe that whole conversation had just taken place. Maybe I was an alcoholic. Jesus. DT's. But if I was an alcoholic, I'd have to stop drinking, wouldn't I? That might be O.K. too. I couldn't imagine ever being able to drink liquor again without puking. I started crying.

Martha came up a few minutes later with some milk and crackers. She stood by the bed looking helpless. Finally she set down the food and took my hand. "Martha?" I mumbled. "Sit with me awhile, please?"

"O.K., Niki." She pulled a chair next to the bed and held my hand until I fell asleep.

Chapter XI

I got up again at two and found a note. "Gone to get your car, try to eat something." I went into the kitchen and found the crackers and some cheese. By concentrating on a bird outside the kitchen window, I managed to choke down a few bites. Then I drank some milk. It was good. I carried the glass into the living room and drank some more. Even though I was still hung over, my brain seemed to have re-engaged itself while I slept. Thank God. That disoriented feeling was terrifying.

The front door slammed, and Martha and Teri came in. "Found a beer," Martha said, holding it up. "Must of rolled out of the six-pack."

"Take it away." I cringed. "I never want to see a can of beer again as long as I live."

"I'll stick it in the fridge," Teri said, carrying it off to the kitchen.

"Is my car O.K.?" I was afraid to look.

"Yeah, it's outside. You must have driven carefully—not a scratch on it. You even switched off your lights." Martha sat down and flipped on the TV set with a remote control device.

"Sure is nice to take the day off," she said. "Between this and my leg, I haven't been in school much."

We stared at a game show, but I was too hyper to watch TV. "Martha, I feel weird."

"What's wrong?" She looked worried. She probably expected me to say the pink elephants dancing on the ceiling were going to fall down on top of me. "I'm uncomfortable with you. It's not Martha and Niki anymore. It's Martha and Niki who Martha thinks is an alcoholic. Do you know what I mean?"

Martha turned off the TV. "You feel isolated?"

"Yeah, exactly. You're really amazing, Martha. You always pick up on what I'm trying to say even if I express it badly."

"Uhm-hmm," Martha said absently. "You're telling me you don't want me to think you're an alcoholic?"

"No . . . well. I want to be Niki to you, not someone else." Especially not someone who terrifies me, I added to myself.

"You are Niki to me, whether you're an alcoholic or not. I can see what you're saying, but most of it is in your own head. If I think you're an alcoholic, it doesn't change you for me. All it means is it'd be better if you didn't drink. If we were at a restaurant, and I ordered a beer and you ordered a Coke, I wouldn't notice. I mean, I wouldn't be saying, "Niki's an alcoholic; she has to order a Coke.""

"But you would notice if I ordered a beer."

Martha thought a little. "That's true, because I'd be worried about what would happen. I'd be worried I might have to get you out of some awful situation. That's what Teri's saying about Al-Anon. If I wasn't afraid I had to take care of you when you're drunk, then I probably wouldn't notice if you ordered a beer either. It wouldn't affect me either way."

"What's Al-Anon?"

"That organization Teri goes to. For friends and relatives of alcoholics."

"Oh," I said. "I just don't want you to think I'm weird."

"Niki, you're not. The problem is *you* think you're weird."

"Jesus, after last night, it's no wonder. Running in front of cars, and fighting with people, and shaking in my sleep."

"Right, but—"

"Hey, Niki," Teri said, reappearing in a clean softball uniform, "you ever hear the phrase 'It's the booze talking'?"

"Yeah."

"Try 'It's the booze acting.' If you started jumping in front of cars stone-cold sober and pushing around Scotty's roommate after a double banana split, I might wonder about your sanity."

"But I'm the same person when I'm drunk. It's me doing all that crazy stuff."

"There's something funny about this crazy business," Martha said. "It's the way you talk about it, only I haven't quite figured it out yet."

"Come on," Teri said. "We have to go. The game starts in twenty minutes."

"I'm not going," I said.

"Why not?" they both asked.

"Because Scotty will be there. I'm too embarrassed."

"Bull," Martha said. "You can't avoid her all your life. Besides, we'll be up in the bleachers."

I was too tired to argue. I went out to the car. It took five minutes to drive to the field, and Teri ran off to join everybody warming up. Martha and I walked slowly to the bleachers, Martha using her cane. I brought along a can of Seven Up because I was still craving fluids.

The game was short, stopped in the fifth inning because Harwood was eleven runs ahead. It was a slaughter, and they were a team we'd beaten easily at the beginning of the season. Martha and I watched the Harwood kids run to their bus screaming with excitement that they'd beaten Lincoln. Our team slunk to the gym.

"I can't stand this," Martha said. "We're totally screwing up. There's only one game left, with Ridgedale. We're not going to make it to the league finals, much less the championship playoffs, and I had all these big fantasies about playing in the state championships this summer. What a joke."

"But if we beat Ridgedale, we go into the league playoffs, don't we? On the basis of our record?"

"Yeah, but we'd lose anyway, so why get all up for the playoffs? Easier just to blow it to Ridgedale." I'd never seen Martha so depressed. She was usually pretty consistent, unlike me.

"Teri's the only one really hitting," I said. "Did you see Sarah only got a single out of three trips to the plate? Against that pitcher?"

"Teri would hit no matter what," Martha said gloomily.

We sat there, so miserable we didn't hear Scotty walk up behind us. "Well, Niki, Martha," she said. I jumped a foot and looked around guiltily. At least the stands were empty.

"I'm surprised to see you here, Niki," she continued. There was an edge to her voice.

I was confused, but Martha bristled immediately. "Why shouldn't she be here?"

"Because she makes Alice nervous, that's why. And I doubt the team wants to see a quitter in the stands."

Silence. I guess Martha was too stunned to think of a comeback. I knew I deserved anything she threw at me, so I kept my mouth shut. But Scotty wasn't finished. "You wanted to say something to me last night. What was it?"

"Nothing," I said. "I don't remember."

"All right," she said and started to walk back to the gym.

But Martha clambered down the bleachers and shouted,

"Hold on, Scotty. You and I have been friends for a long time. Don't pull any teacher authority trip on me. I don't see why you're picking on Niki. The only reason we were a championship team in the first place—"

"I don't need to pull any authority trip, Martha. Look at the facts. Teri is sitting up there crying because we lost the game, and she spent all last night running around taking care of Niki. And we lose you, defending Niki in a fight. And Niki, who is the best pitcher in the league, quits because she's too selfish and immature to recognize she has a problem and deal with it like an adult. And don't tell me Niki's pitching made us a championship team. Sure, that was a big part of it, but a team is a team, and when the individual parts stop working, the whole team suffers. No individual made this team champion."

"And," Martha flashed, "no individual is tearing it apart now."

Scotty turned to me. "I'll say this for you, Niki. You manage to surround yourself with loyal friends. Can't you speak for yourself?"

I blinked at her, mumbling a couple of "pardon me's" while I climbed down the wooden rows. The instant my feet hit solid earth, I bolted off across the field to the parking lot, leaving Martha hollering behind me. Everything Scotty said was true. I was a rotten apple, wrecking everybody merely by existing. The only decent thing to do was disappear. Why had I even come to the game? I sprinted around the corner by the lot and saw Frank starting up his old car. "Frank!" I shouted. "Wait." When I got to his door, I said, "Frank, would you take me to Teri's? My car's there."

"Sure," he said. "Hop in. What's the matter?"

"Nothing," I said. "I'm just in a rush. I have to go up to the university to see one of the professors." The lie flowed so easily

97

I was shocked. See, I thought, you really are a schmuck. Frank drove fast and dropped me off at the car. "Thanks," I shouted as he pulled away.

Now what, smartass? I got in my car and started it. Martha would be worried, I realized. That wasn't fair—she'd been through enough. I grabbed a sheet of notebook paper and wrote, "Martha. I've gone down to Carmel. See you soon." It wasn't much, but I figured it would do. I pinned it on Teri's door, drove to the liquor store, and cashed a check for all but five dollars of my summer savings. Then I started driving south. I stopped at a gas station about seventy miles away and called my house. Joyce answered. "Hi, Mom?"

"Niki?"

"Mom, I need to get away for a couple of days. I need to think."

She didn't say anything for a minute, digesting the fact I'd called her "mom." "Niki, what's wrong?"

"I don't know," I said honestly. "I think it will help to go to Carmel. I'll be at Davenport's. You can call anytime. I've got the car and some money. I'll be back Monday."

"But what about school? Don't you have finals?"

"No, I finished all of them." Actually that wasn't true. I had a chemistry test on Friday.

"But, Niki . . ." She paused, and I didn't say anything either. I watched the cars going by on the freeway, waiting for her to make up her mind. "Will you be careful?" She sounded plaintive, and I almost blurted it all out to her, about the team and Scotty and the blackouts.

Instead I said, "Yes, I'll be careful. I swear I will."

"I wish you'd talked to us about this. Maybe we could help."

"I'll talk to you when I get back," I promised. "But I need to be alone first."

"All right," she said. "Niki, you know your father and I love you."

"I know. I love you too."

I was grateful; she seemed to have understood. I drove on, trying not to think, but I couldn't stop my head from foaming as hard as the ocean I was traveling to see. Why do I keep screwing up? Why do I mess up everybody's life? My intentions are good, but along the way I discover I've been transformed into a selfish creep. I must really be a creep. The only answer was to search for that kid who stood on the cliff five years ago. I wasn't sure why I'd lost her, but I was going to try like hell to bring her back to life.

I was totally exhausted when I checked into Davenport's Motel. I realized I hadn't eaten anything for hours, maybe even days. I went up to the restaurant and ordered a bowl of soup. That went down O.K., and I tried a salad. Even better. Then I ordered a cheeseburger. It was too much, and I left half on my plate and went to bed.

I got up early the next morning and drove to the ocean. I clambered up to the cliffs and felt lonely, not proud. I'd escaped here, running from the mess I'd made at home. I poked around in the tide pools for an hour or so and climbed up and down rocks, but after a while I admitted I was kidding myself. There was nothing for me here, no great hope answered. I was turning into a woman I couldn't recognize, and I carried her every place I went. I was scared to death of myself. I went to a liquor store and bought a couple of bottles of gin and a case of beer.

I drank, but I couldn't seem to get drunk. Or maybe I was drunk, because I lost track of the hours, but I never got happy or even angry-proud. I just stayed depressed, and after a while I realized I was incredibly lonely. I wanted to go back home, but I knew I'd make even more of a mess. I'd backed myself into a corner, trapped myself behind a wall I couldn't climb over. My parents would want to know why I'd gone off, and what could I tell them? Martha and Teri were probably sick to death of me, and Scotty hated me. Chuck had given up months ago. The worst thing was it was my fault, but I didn't know how to make things right. I seemed to have a real knack for hurting everybody I loved. I got up and paced around. Finally I got tired of thinking and turned on the TV.

Chapter XII

I woke up to the noise of a game show and pounding. I flipped off the TV, and the pounding continued. Someone's at the door, I thought, and I looked around at the mess of beer cans and a half-empty gin bottle. Oh, who cares?

I threw open the door and Martha stood there, acting sheepish. I was so happy to see her I could hardly speak.

"I figured you'd be here," she said. "Can I come in?"

"Yes, yes. God, I'm glad to see you."

"You are? I was afraid you'd be angry."

"No, no, I thought I'd given up . . . but when I saw you . . ."

"O.K.," Martha said.

"How'd you get here?"

"Your parents called me. They were worried. They offered to pay my bus fare down. I said no. I knew you wanted to be alone, but then I decided, hell, I'm bored, so I came down."

I looked at her.

"That's not entirely true. But I didn't want you to think I was checking up on you, and I *was* bored."

"Never mind, as long as you're here. What's today?"

"Friday. Now, I want you to get one thing straight. I'm here for myself, not for you. And I'm not checking up. I'm not going to make one comment about this"—she waved her arm—"incredible clutter of beer cans and bottles and the fact that you are obviously planning to drink yourself to death, which I personally find melodramatic."

"O.K., Martha," I said, laughing. "I'm glad you're not going to comment on that. How did you come to all these conclusions?"

"I've just spent the last day and a half at about a hundred meetings of A.A. and Al-Anon. I realized I had to find some way to deal with your drinking if I wanted to continue being friends with you. So I am no longer concerning myself with any aspect of your drinking, taking care of you, protecting you, or doing things for you that are your responsibility."

"That sounds fair and good." In a way, it was a relief. Martha still wanted to be my friend, and I didn't have to worry about messing her up with my drinking. But on the other hand, it made me feel twice as lonely. I didn't say that, though. I figured that was my problem.

"By the way, I went to your teachers, and I guess you're all done except for the chemistry final, which is today and is open-book. Old What's-His-Name gave me the exam and said for you to have it in on Monday. That's what the rest of the class is doing, only he gave it to me Thursday instead of today. I told him you were having a nervous breakdown."

"Thanks, Martha. You're a great press agent. But if you're not protecting me, how come you're running around to all my teachers, bringing me my chem final, and tripping down here on a Greyhound in the first place?"

"You weren't supposed to notice that," Martha said. "Hey, is there any food in this joint, or are you on a strictly liquid diet?"

I laughed honestly, a big hearty laugh that relaxed me a little. God, to finally be able to laugh! Maybe life wasn't so bad after all. "Come on," I said, "I'll buy you breakfast."

I ate two plates of eggs, bacon, and pancakes, drank four glasses of orange juice, two of milk, and three cups of coffee. Martha nibbled, by comparison, on ham and eggs, no toast. Then we went down to the beach and settled our blankets next to the river that flooded into the ocean. Lying on my back, looking out at the waves, I felt pretty good.

"Hey, Martha. Do your moods swing all over the place? I mean, you wanta kill yourself one day and the next you feel great?"

"No, not really. I've never seriously considered suicide. Sometimes I get upset about something, like the team losing, but I'm usually pretty steady."

I flopped over on my stomach. "Are you ever worried about yourself? Scared of yourself?"

"I get scared, but not of myself."

I looked at the sand. It was all dark under my shadow. "Coming here didn't work. I brought myself with me."

Martha plowed up a miniature furrow in the beach with her finger. "You remember when you said drinking keeps you sane, like releasing steam in a pressure cooker?"

"Yeah."

"Now you think you're nuts, but it doesn't have anything to do with drinking, right?"

I nodded. "It's as if these crazy things I do when I'm drunk are crowded under the surface, waiting to pop out when I let go a little. Then there are the mood jumps and depressions. I'm . . . all melancholy. That doesn't have anything to do with drinking."

"But look at what you're saying. First drinking was keeping you sane, and now you're insane and drinking isn't the prob- lem. The only logic that runs through that is that your drinking is acceptable. You're protecting your drinking. You're willing to call yourself crazy and be miserable so you can keep right on boozing."

I thought about it. "No, Martha, I don't see that. Drinking helps because I get less scared of myself when I drink. I feel good about myself. Sometimes," I added, remembering last night.

"But it's a vicious circle, Niki! You black out and you get completely disoriented and wander around in this daze. And you do all these dumb things when you're drunk, and you hate yourself for them. But because you don't want to stop drinking, you put the blame for all that bad stuff on you—not on the booze that's making you be crazy in the first place. You ought to be scared of alcohol, Niki, not yourself."

I shrugged. "I don't know, Martha. Let's stop talking about it, O.K.?" But I was depressed. What if she was right? I would have to stop drinking. But I knew I couldn't stop drinking. No way in hell could I stop. So what would I do? I got a hollow feeling in the pit of my stomach, in spite of all the food I'd eaten. I was scared. Martha couldn't help. She thought it was easy, all I had to do was stop. I was alone again, and I didn't like myself. It frightened me so much I almost started crying. I got up quickly. "I'm going to take a walk," I said.

"O.K." Martha readjusted her sunglasses and settled across the sand. I hated her for a moment, lying there so comfortably. But it wasn't her fault. I started walking, my mind working furiously. Lately, on mornings when I woke up sober, even when I hadn't had one beer the night before, I'd go through the events of the past evening compulsively, making sure I hadn't forgotten anything. While I was doing it, I'd keep saying to myself, You didn't drink! Of course you remember everything! Only I couldn't seem to get out of bed before I went through the whole process. And the guilt, Jesus Christ, the guilt! Even if

104

nothing horrible had happened, I'd wake up wishing somebody would throw me against a few walls, punish me somehow for being such an awful person. I was perpetually apologetic. Sure, walk right over me, I deserve it. Could all that be from drinking? But if it was, what could I do about it? I was addicted to liquor the same way I was to cigarettes. I'd been making jokes about it since I was fourteen. "Oh, no," I'd say when somebody would offer me some reds or speed, "I'm already hooked on booze and cigarettes. That's plenty for me." And everyone would laugh. Ha, ha.

Very funny. Very fucking funny. My mouth worked a little, and I had to blink tears back. Jesus, I was a mess! Trudging along the beach crying. I went back to the blanket and flopped down beside Martha. She was asleep. I got up again and paced around. Why was I so nervous? I sat down and read the questions for my chemistry final. Two of them were easy, and I wrote them out in my notebook. I forced myself to work out the answer to a third. Then I put everything away and watched the ocean. Look how immense the ocean is, I told myself soothingly. All that incredible power, going on and on, even if nobody was here to see it. . . . Was that what I thought about when I was twelve? Does a tree falling in a deserted forest make any noise? Oh, I was a bright one, all right. I stood up, disgusted with myself. O.K., genius, how about a picnic lunch? Martha might like that. She hadn't eaten much breakfast.

I drove up to the little imported foods market and spent a pretty happy half-hour choosing cheeses and meats for sandwiches. Then I bought a loaf of French bread and two sixpacks of beer. I went back to the beach. Martha was still asleep. A little disappointing, but all right. I put the beer in the river and the food under a bush. Then I had another good idea. I'd go swimming. I tore off my pants and tennis shoes and dove in. I started prowling around near the sand bars, chasing the sea gulls. After a while, I heard Martha calling me. "Niki, c'mere!"

I pulled my pants on over my wet underwear and left my shoes by the beer. "I woke up when I heard people yelling. Look out there. Seals!"

The seals were playing in the waves, leaping around, popping up here and there, rolling on their backs until another seal got too close. Then keep-away, dive, down into the surf. "I wish I was a seal," I said, and the minute the words were out of my mouth, I was depressed again. Damn.

"Hey, Martha. You hungry? I got some cheese and salami and stuff."

"Oh, good! Boy, this is so much better than hanging around school. I think it's criminal people have to go to school. Everybody ought to be able to lie around all day on the beach."

"Yeah, but then the beaches would be mobbed with packs of bored, restless people."

"You're such a pessimist. Hand me the French bread."

We sat down and started eating. Martha didn't say anything about the beer, following her new formula. I ate only one sandwich, but Martha was ravenous. She practically shoveled her way through half the loaf of bread. "God, I'm stuffed!" she moaned. "Ugh! And I can't even run it off."

"How's your leg?"

"It's better. I don't have to use the cane except to go up and down steps." She opened up a fresh beer and sipped at it. "This is absolutely fantastic. You picked a nice place to run to. I'll give you that. You could have hidden out at some fleabag hotel in the Tenderloin. By the way, Scotty wants to talk to you when you come back."

I'm not coming back, I thought, but I said, "What does she want?"

106

"I think she wants to apologize. She was upset she said that, about you being a quitter and all the rest. She probably lost the allocation. Did I tell you that already? She heard it's pretty much down the drain. She was hoping to get some sort of financial aid through the conference, but her request was turned down. It was the end of the line. Teri said she walked into the locker room, saw half the team crying, and tore back out again."

"That's not a good excuse, though I suppose she has the right to fly off the handle even if she is a teacher. Especially when everything she said was true."

"Oh, Niki! You're not selfish. In a lot of ways, you're one of the most generous people I know. It all goes back to the same thing. When you're protecting your drinking or you're drunk, you *are* selfish and impossible. Sometimes I'd like to strangle you, especially when you're acting king of the mountain, expecting everybody to fall at your feet praising you. But usually you're fine. Scotty realized that."

"But Martha, I'm *still* drinking! I haven't stopped. See." I gulped at my beer. "You act as if everything's great. Scotty's going to apologize, and you're going to Al-Anon— Oh, I don't know what I'm trying to say."

"Nothing's changed for you, right?"

"Right."

Martha sighed. "Since I went to all those meetings and figured out the craziness business, I can separate you better from your drinking. But that doesn't mean you stopped. You're still right in the middle of it, no matter what I see."

I nodded miserably. "Anyway," I said, "I don't believe any of that stuff about the craziness. Everybody drinks. I just have to be careful. It's probably because my parents drink so much. I grew up with the wrong attitude."

Martha didn't say anything. She lazily opened a beer. "My God," I said. "Four beers. A record."

"Uhm-hmm," she said, only she couldn't finish it. She gave half to me.

Three hours and eight beers later, we were back at the motel. I strolled into the kitchenette. I was feeling pretty grown up, walking in from a picnic on the beach on Friday, no one to answer to, the fixings for drinks in the refrigerator. Just like adults. Well, seventeen is adult enough. "Hey Martha! You want a gin and tonic?"

"What?" she yelled from the shower.

"I say, Do you want a gin and tonic?"

But Martha spoiled the image. "No, all that beer and sun gave me a headache. I'm going to lie down awhile."

"All right," I said and gloomily went back to the kitchen to mix my own drink. But my mood went up again when I looked across the court and saw some people playing pool in the little rec room. I sauntered over in my bare feet, drink in hand. "Can I challenge the table?"

A man in a blue workshirt stopped racking the balls and looked me up and down. "Sure, toss in your quarter."

I stuck a quarter under the bank and sipped at my drink. The men played quickly, and I was up. They were much better than I was, but who cared? This was a vacation. I could do anything I wanted.

I racked the balls and stepped aside. The man in the workshirt broke. "Whatcha drinkin' there, sweetie?"

"Gin and tonic," I answered.

"Wanta play for a drink in the bar at the restaurant?"

"Sure, why not?"

I shot down two solids. It was amazing how booze did away with my nervousness. It seemed I could do everything better drunk. Shoot better pool, tell funny stories.

"You're a pretty good shot," the man said.

"I've been playing awhile."

He whipped down four stripes and barely missed a fifth.

"Looks like I better get my ass in gear," I said. I sighted one ball. It looked pretty easy. It fell with a hollow plunk. My next shot missed, but it caromed off the bank and knocked one in anyway. I pretended I planned it that way. Then I smashed in another. "Hey, sweetie," Workshirt said. "You goin' to college around here?"

"No," I snapped. He'd broken my concentration. I missed the next shot.

"You live around here?"

"No."

"How old are you?"

"Seventeen," I said without thinking. He just looked at me, and his friend laughed. He shot down his remaining balls and plonked in the eight. "I'll take a rain check on the drink, kid. When you're legal."

"Screw you," I said and left before he could say anything. I stormed back into the motel room. Martha was asleep again. "Goddamn!" I said under my breath. I went into the kitchen and began working on my chemistry final, drinking gin and tonics while I did it. When my writing got so scrawled I couldn't read it, I gave up. I staggered into the front room. Martha was reading. "Well, hi," I said.

"Hi, Niki. You know, I feel lousy. Too much sun."

"That's too bad," I said.

"But I'm a little hungry. Are you?" She looked up from the book at me slumped in the armchair.

I tinkled the ice in the glass. "Liquid diet, remember? But there's still stuff from lunch. You want something?"

"Yeah, just cheese, O.K.? That meat's too fatty."

I went into the kitchen and hacked off pieces of bread and cheese. I arranged it on a plate, holding one eye shut so I could see where the plate was. Then back in. "Service for a queen," I said.

She started eating, reading her book at the same time. I

109

picked up a magazine, but I couldn't focus on the page. I was bored. "Martha, let's do something."

"Like what?"

"I don't know. Play cards or drive around."

"No, I don't feel like driving and you're too drunk. And I'm tired. I want to read."

"But I'm bored."

"Niki, I'm sorry. I don't want to do anything."

I stumbled back into the kitchen and fixed another drink. Then I decided I actually wanted a beer, so I gulped down the drink and got a beer. I was having trouble walking. I fell against the door going back in the front room. Martha glanced up at me and started reading again.

"Hey, Martha. Is this your new system? Ignore me?"

"You're not exactly scintillating when you're falling all over yourself and you can hardly talk."

"You think I'm disgusting, huh?"

"You're trying to start a fight because you're bored. Why don't you pass out or take a cold shower or something?"

"You're a real creep, Martha. I was fine till you came. What gives you the right to come here and think I'm disgusting and put me down and stuff?"

Martha didn't answer. "Well?" I shouted. "Tell me!"

"Teri was right," Martha said. "She said I shouldn't come. There's no way of being with you without getting involved in your drinking. And maybe you are drinking more because I'm here. I'm leaving tomorrow."

The way she said it scared me, so I yelled at her. "Good riddance! I don't want you here anyway!" I pulled my wallet out of my pants. "Here! Money for the bus. Go on, take it!"

"I'm paying my own way back," she said, keeping her eyes stubbornly on the book.

"No you're not! I won't let you." I threw a ten-dollar bill on the page she was reading, and she grabbed it and threw it back. "God damn it, Niki, would you leave me alone? We'll talk about it in the morning, when you can think!"

"We'll talk about it now," I yelled, and I grabbed her by the front of her tee shirt.

She looked up, startled, and the fear on her face gave me a thrill, as if I had control over her. I threw myself on her, pinning her down with my knees. "Niki, get off!"

"Martha, I don't want you ever saying I'm disgusting."

"I didn't say it, you did, stupid! Now get off me!"

"But you think it. I know you do! You think you're so cool, and I'm this drunken, disgusting idiot that oughta be locked up. I know you, Martha. I know you think that!"

Martha heaved me over and tried to scramble off the bed, but she was too slow with her leg. She turned and threw up her arm as I caught up with her. I grabbed her arm and slapped her hard across the face, once, twice, and she tumbled back on the bed, still fighting. I held her down and slapped her again and again, watching her cry, watching blood start trickling down her chin from the corner of her mouth. I couldn't hear anything, and time seemed to have stopped. But finally I heard Martha calling from a long way off, "Niki, please stop, Niki."

Martha. That was Martha in trouble. I came to and realized what I was doing, who I was slapping, and I stared at my hands like they were killers. "My God," I screamed. "My God, I'm a monster! Oh, my God!" I slammed my hands against the wall, trying to break them, separate them from the rest of me, and the whole time I was beating the wall, I heard this eerie crying, like a heartbroken woman wailing for the dead. When I realized it was me making the noise, I passed out.

Chapter XIII

I moaned when I turned over on my hand. I dragged it out from under the blanket and looked at it. The knuckles were big and bleeding. I could hardly move my fingers. And my left hand was nearly as bad. I closed my eyes, lying there suspended. . . . Then I remembered. The floor, the bed, everything shot from under me, and I yelled for Martha. I scrabbled my hand into a vast empty space. I staggered out of bed, tripped on the covers, fell to my knees, got back up, and ran to the kitchen. The bread sat wrapped on a shelf. I stumbled back into the front room. My head was pounding. The table she'd put her suitcase on was empty. I stared at it, blinking. Toothbrush. If she hasn't taken her toothbrush, she's still here. I ran into the bathroom. My new toothbrush sat by itself in the holder. I stared, speechless, motionless, and then a dam burst in me, and I crumpled to the cold floor, sobbing, "Martha, don't do this to me, don't leave me. God, I'm sorry, don't leave me alone, I can't stand to be alone!"

A hurricane was blowing through my head, drowning everything out. Something lifted me, and a cold river drove into my face. I was drowning, I struggled to get out. . . . Martha was holding me. "Niki, it's all right. I'm here. You're O.K."

"Martha, Martha, thank God you're here. Is it you?" I pulled away and stared at her. She was crying.

"Niki, come here, honey, get off the floor. Come on, get on the bed."

"I'm all wet."

"I threw some water on you. You were screaming."

"Martha, I thought, I thought you'd left. Did you leave?"

"Yes. But I came back. Last night when you were hitting me, you kept yelling, 'Drunk, drunk,' with this terrible hatred, and you were hitting yourself, Niki. I couldn't leave. I thought when you woke up you might kill yourself. I wanted to tell you—" But she couldn't finish.

"Oh, Martha, please don't cry. I can't stand it. God, I'm such a monster. I don't know. Nothing's bad enough. . . . Martha, I've gotta get help!" We held each other, both of us crying, trying to comfort the other. I held her face between my hands and looked at her. "Martha, it doesn't even matter if you hate me. I can't live like this, hating myself this way. It's— Something's changed. I have to stop. Oh, God, I've got to be honest if I'm going to live. Martha, I have to stop drinking. It's driving me crazy and hurting you, and . . . Oh, God!"

Martha rocked me back and forth while I clung to her. "I can't help you, Niki. You see that, don't you? I'd give anything if I could, but I can't."

"I know, I know," I moaned. "But what if I can't stop drinking? I've got to. I'll go crazy. This can't keep happening. If it goes on, I'll die!"

"Niki, Niki . . ."

"Martha, will Teri take me to an A.A. meeting?"

"Yes."

"It's got to work. It has to. Martha, I'm an alcoholic."

She didn't answer. She held me, and relief spread through me like warm water, and I knew I wasn't crazy. I didn't have to fight anymore. I relaxed in her arms, and when I slumped down, Martha got a towel and dried off my face. "It doesn't matter anymore, Martha, but I guess you hate me now."

"No, I don't hate you. I realized last night I couldn't do anything for you. I was making things worse. I gave up. But I wanted to try to tell you one last time not to hate yourself."

"Martha, I'm not insane. I'm just an alcoholic."

"I know, Niki, I know. That's what I've been trying to tell you. But you couldn't hear me."

"Why was it so hard to see? I don't understand."

"Because you didn't want to stop drinking. It was even more important than you. And it was a million times more important than me. I couldn't compete with that."

"Martha, I feel good, but I feel scared. Like I'm finally doing something right, but it means all these heavy changes. What if I can't do it?"

"Don't worry about that now. Everything will take care of itself. Do you want to go back?"

"Yes, but I want to call Teri first."

"It's only eight-thirty, but, oh, go ahead."

The phone rang six times, and then I heard Teri's sleepy voice.

"Teri, would you take me to an A.A. meeting sometime? I mean, that's not what I want to say. Would you take me to one today?"

"There's one at noon, Niki. You can make it up by then. Come to my house."

"Thanks, Teri."

"Hey, Niki? I'm glad. Say hello to Martha for me."

We paid the bill and got on the road. Martha drove. I was

114

too shaky. We didn't talk much, but Martha reached over and squeezed my shoulder a couple of times. I felt as if we were racing home to the future, the way I expected to feel driving to Carmel to stand on the cliffs. But this time I was running toward, instead of running away.

Chapter XIV

Teri was sitting outside on the porch reading when we pulled up. The first thing she noticed were my hands. "Jeez, Niki, how're you going to pitch Wednesday?"

"Pitch?" I echoed stupidly. Then I realized I was going off to A.A., exactly the way Scotty wanted. But pitching was the furthest thing from my mind. I had to find a way to live with myself. I didn't care anymore that I was a star pitcher. I didn't care about anything except escaping this rat maze. I turned to Martha. "Listen," I said, "I'm sorry, but I don't want you to come. It'll be bad enough already. I mean—"

"Never mind," Martha said. "That's O.K. Drop me off on your way."

"Can we take your car, Teri? I'm too shaky to drive. And my hands are killing me."

"How 'bout I drive yours, Niki? My parents are back, and they do the grocery shopping on Saturday."

"That's fine, as long as I don't have to drive."

We let Martha out at her house, and then much too soon Teri pulled into a space. I was losing all my resolve to fear. "Teri, do I have to say I'm an alcoholic?"

"You don't have to say anything. You don't have to sign anything or join. All you have to do is sit there and listen."

"All right," I said. "I guess I can do that." We got out of the car and climbed some rickety steps. I heard voices at the top. I moved closer to Teri as we entered the main room. Nothing happened. People kept right on talking. What'd you expect, stupid? I snarled at myself. Applause? I shook my head. I wished my brain would start working right again.

I was too scared to look at anyone. Teri introduced me to some younger women, but I could only mumble and turn away. Finally one of them asked me if it was my first meeting. "Yeah," I said. "I told Teri I'd come with her a couple of times."

She smiled as if she knew what I really meant. "I was so scared the first five meetings I don't remember anything that happened. I was sitting in this big cloud of absolute terror."

I looked at her gratefully. "I'm pretty scared," I admitted. "And, uh, I feel awful. I have this horrible hangover."

She smiled. "That's O.K. Most people coming here for the first time have horrible hangovers. It's natural, since all of us are alcoholics."

I looked at the floor. "Yeah, I guess so. Could I tell you what I did last night? I'm pretty upset about it."

"Sure, we have a few minutes before the meeting starts. Come and sit over here." She led me to a couch, and I launched into my story. "I have to stop doing these crazy numbers," I finished. "Poor Martha—"

"Forget Martha," the woman said. "She'll take care of herself. You worry about *you*. Look, everybody's done some awful things. They fade with time and sobriety. It's an incredible relief to know you never have to do those things again. That's what's scary—when you know you'll keep right on doing them, no matter how much you don't want to."

"I know, I know. That's what I'm going through now."

"Look," she said. "You probably didn't catch my name. It's Mandy." She wrote down her phone number for me. "Call any time you want. And get some more numbers in case people aren't home."

"O.K.," I said, pocketing the slip of paper. A bell rang. People started moving into the meeting room. I looked around frantically for Teri.

She materialized at my elbow. "Remember, you don't have to say anything if you don't want to."

"All right," I said. I was scared, but I followed her in. I was willing to do anything as long as I could stop feeling this way.

When I got back home, I had to deal with my parents. After the initial flurry of hugs and "Thank goodness you're safe" they wanted to know what was the matter with me. And what on earth had happened to my hands? While I spun a little tale about slipping on the jagged cliffs at the beach, I debated inside what to tell them. I suspected they wouldn't be exactly thrilled I was an alcoholic. In fact, they might have a real fit, and I felt too raw and new to defend myself against a bunch of arguments. I told them I couldn't talk about it yet, but I had figured stuff out—the trip had worked. I promised I'd explain everything soon. They weren't very happy, but they were impressed I was being honest and telling them anything at all. "We're here to help, Niki," my mother said. Though Carl nodded in agreement, I knew he was secretly relieved he didn't have to hear my explanation right then and there. He needed more time to digest the idea that his perfect, sensible daughter might have a flaw.

I tried sitting with them during cocktail hour and dinner, but it was too hard. I went back to my staying in my room routine, telling them I was making plans for a new emphasis and layout for the sports page next year. They didn't believe me, but I didn't know what else to say. They knew I'd finished all my school work. Sunday night, when they thought I was asleep, I heard my father's worried cough, the one he always uses when he's about to bring up something difficult. "This seems to be more than the usual teenage depression."

"Of course it is," my mother said. "It's this town. Everything happens too fast. Why must she go to college a year early? Senior year is the best."

"She hasn't been accepted yet," Carl pointed out.

"She will be." Silence. I was glad Joyce was so positive I'd be accepted. I could hear her sigh, then continue. "Whatever is worrying her is reflected in the amount she drinks. I'm serious, Carl." My father had probably made a face. "Haven't you noticed how much gin and beer she consumes? I do the shopping, so I know. You start giving her wine when she's fourteen—"

"Let's not go through that again. European kids are practically weaned on wine. She's gotten drunk a few times, we all overdid it when the Kitchells were here, but she is basically a very sensible girl. Would you rather she was out partying with her friends, getting into a lot of trouble in the process? Remember how she and Martha left before the police busted up that madhouse at Roger Hickman's. We live in a drinking world. She's been raised in a culture that actually sets aside specific events where drunkenness is not only acceptable but almost required—New Year's Eve, college reunions, Saturday night."

My mother's hiss was so low I could barely hear her. "Don't lecture me. What alternative did we offer her, Carl? When she was a child, did we take her skiing or camping or boating? How did she see us having fun with *our* friends? At cocktail parties, three-bottle bridge nights, and champagne breakfasts.

Don't be hypocritical about *our* society. We're a part of it."

I pictured the astonishment on my father's face. He, after all, was a cosmopolitan, as far removed from the barroom crowd as a cave dweller from Buckingham Palace. Three-martini lunches don't count when they're tax deductible. He recovered quickly. "We can't shield Niki. She's almost eighteen. She has to know how to handle herself."

"Why?" Joyce wailed, back to her previous complaint. "Why does everything have to move so fast? When I was eighteen, I didn't have to choose between birth control pills and Quaaludes, or chablis and angel dust!"

"The drugs might be new, but nothing else is. Why do you suppose the Japanese bombed Pearl Harbor on Sunday morning?"

I smiled into my pillow. That line was Carl's show stopper whenever he bemoaned America's woefully immature attitude toward alcohol. My mother had heard it a million times. "Oh, *Carl!* " she said, her voice leaden with scorn.

"Look," he countered. "We've gotten way off the subject here. Her drinking isn't the problem. We can't know what the matter is until she tells us. She said the trip was a success."

"Then why hasn't she spoken more than three words to us since she's been back? Why does she hide in her room all evening?"

"I have no idea. I don't like it any more than you do. It could be something as simple as loneliness. Aren't teenagers always lonely?" He said it as if anyone below the age of twenty was a strange species of jungle gorilla.

"*Everyone* is always lonely," my mother snapped. That remark ended their discussion. I heard my father plod downstairs and my mother go to the bathroom. All the Etchens off on their separate tanker journeys.

I switched on my headboard light and sat up in bed, running through their conversation piece by piece. I was surprised at a number of things. How had my mother heard of angel dust? But that was the least of the questions. For some reason, it had never occurred to me that Joyce replaced the gin and beer I drank, although occasionally I would slip a six-pack in the bar refrigerator, and I had the perpetual bottle in my room. She had actually wondered about my drinking! And she was dead right about my upbringing. I remembered carrying to school a lunchbox full of leftover cocktail party hors d'oeuvres instead of a tuna sandwich like everyone else. I was *very* mature that day, nibbling on my smoked oysters. If anyone had asked me what adults did for entertainment, I would have unhesitatingly answered, "Drink."

The best part, I realized, was that my mother might support me when I told them about my alcoholism. It was clear I was going to have to say something soon. They were hurt and worried. It wasn't fair to keep them on tenterhooks, and I didn't want to lie. As I fell asleep, I was hopeful, and that in itself was a big step forward.

By Monday I was feeling pretty good. A couple days not drinking worked wonders. I crouched forward, my glove on my swollen hand, squinting in the sun. The pitcher threw an easy one in, and the girl at bat cracked it my way. I scooped it up and made a good throw to first. But the first baseman couldn't hold on to it. The batter made it to second. I shook my head. I wished I'd hear from the university soon. I couldn't stand the idea of going through a year of regular high school P.E. Maybe I could take something interesting, like fencing or sailing.

"Niki!"

I looked over at Mrs. Michaels. Scotty was standing next to her. I trotted off the field. "Go on in, Jenkins," Mrs. Michaels said to a tall skinny girl. "Miss McDougall wants to talk to you," she said.

"Hi, Scotty."

"Hi, Niki."

We looked at each other. "Uh, why don't we go sit over there," Scotty motioned, walking toward a deserted strip of grass. Once we'd sat down, Scotty stared ahead of her for a moment and said, "Niki, I wanted to tell you I was sorry I said all that . . . garbage the other day. I was upset about various things, but there's no justification—"

I cut into her speech. "I never apologized to you or your roommate for rampaging through your house last week. That stunt still makes me low man on the totem pole."

Scotty smiled. "Martha said you went to A.A. Saturday."

"That's right. Martha has a big mouth. Did she tell you why?"

"No, though she mentioned you'd hurt your hands. Let me see."

I displayed my hands. They didn't look too bad, but the knuckles were sore. "I think she told me," Scotty said, "because she was afraid you wouldn't, and she figured you'd want to pitch against Ridgedale Wednesday."

"I didn't go to A.A. so I could pitch in the game."

"I know you didn't, Niki, but I'm glad you did anyway, whatever reason you had. Now, if you want to pitch—"

"Scotty, wait, I want to say something. I don't want to pitch in the game just because I went to A.A. I don't think you should have made going to A.A. a condition of my staying on the team. It's my health; you can't make things right or wrong for me. You should have either thrown me off the team or let me stay. If I came back and pitched now, it'd be like agreeing with your doing it in the first place. I won't do that."

Scotty twisted a bit of grass in her fingers. "Is that what you were coming over to tell me last week?"

I laughed. "Probably. Though I don't think I would have made any sense. I suppose I would have ended up screaming obscenities at you or something. It's lucky you were gone."

Scotty turned over on her stomach. "I have to swallow my pride and admit you're right. I've been talking to Teri. She told me trying to force you to go to A.A. was the worst possible way to approach it. Martha was close when she talked about the teacher authority trip. I have a friend who drinks heavily. I can't do anything about her so I ended up taking my frustrations out on you. I'm sorry."

"Well, I got there anyway, so it's no big deal. Now it's my turn to swallow my pride. I would love to pitch in that game. O.K.?"

Scotty smiled. "O.K., Niki. Come on, let's go. Oh, Mrs. Michaels, Niki is moving back over to my class. I'll fill out the papers, so don't worry about it. All right?"

Mrs. Michaels waved us away wearily. She shouted something, but neither of us could hear. "Probably something about thirty girls, and every one of them has to play."

"Yeah. And that'll be me next year."

What a bummer for Scotty to teach a regular P.E. class! "Hey, Scotty, Frank suggested to me a while ago that we organize a car wash and a dance and raise some money for the women's team. He said the boys on their team would help. We could do it in the fall."

Scotty scowled. "It infuriates me that we would have to hold a dance to keep the only women's athletic activity alive. But I guess humility can go a long way."

"For the sophomores," I said nobly. "They didn't get to play much this year."

Scotty looked at me out of the corner of her eye as I laughed. "Unh-hunh! Lessee, there's nine juniors and four sophomores on this team. Of course, since you're being so generous, we could keep you on as an adviser to Alice. You could shout directions from the dugout."

123

"Right," I said. "I'd be great at that. No, I must admit I have a little vested interest in this car-wash business. I'll be out there slinging the sponges harder than anyone."

We reached the warm-up area where Alice was pitching to Sarah. Sarah rose out of her crouch as we approached. "Well," she said, "the great white wonder decides she isn't too busy to pitch the last game! How exciting! You want us to strew roses—"

"Hold on, Sarah," Scotty said.

"No, wait, let me explain, Scotty. I never was too busy. Scotty and I were having a disagreement as to whether I was going to go to Alcoholics Anonymous or not. We couldn't see eye to eye, and I quit. All that's settled so I'm back."

Sarah stared at me a second and then grinned. "O.K., sorry, Niki. I should have realized it was something else. You wanta warm up?"

I waved my fingers around. "No, tell you what, Sarah. I'll give Alice a few more pointers, and if you don't mind, we could come out at lunch tomorrow. That and the warm-up Wednesday ought to get me back in shape."

Sarah nodded. "That's fine. I'm really up for this game. You want to practice till ten Tuesday night it's O.K. with me."

Chapter XV

It was a good thing Sarah and I went out at lunch Tuesday, because my hands were still sore, and I had to make a few alterations in my delivery. By game time the whole team was incredibly high. Scotty kept trying to calm everyone down. "Look," she said, "you're all going to swing at the first three pitches even if they're in the dirt, you're so damned nervous. Cool it. It's only another ball game."

Teri tossed a ball in the air and circled under it. "Sure," she said. "Just another game. Last of the season and the clincher. I can't wait to get at those West Bay and Central champions."

"Let's win this game first," Sarah warned. "If we look ahead too much, we're going to blow this one."

"That's right," Martha put in. "And who wants that creep Julie Baxter going to the playoffs instead of us, eh? Remember that, everybody."

"Too bad you can't play," I said to her as we took the field.

"I'll be O.K.," Martha said. "You know what, Niki? I've decided we don't have enough confidence in each other. We worry too much."

"Hmmm. You're probably right. You notice anything funny

about anybody's batting while you're watching, tell me. O.K.?"

Martha nodded and clapped me on the back. "Strike 'em out, kiddo. You do all the work. That way they sure as hell can't get a run."

It took me a walk and a base hit to settle down to business. Sarah gave me the high sign, and I slung in a fastball. Then my sinker, and a high and outside. The batter figured it was the sinker and swung way low. One out. Then Julie was up, fourth position. I struck her out, and she gave me such a look of hatred I felt a shiver run across my shoulders. Stupid, I thought. Get yourself together. But her whole scene bothered me. She played for life and death. The last batter popped up, and our right fielder ran in and snatched it for once. We were up and running.

By the fourth inning, we had a three-run lead, which I wasn't too happy about, but it was better than nothing. My hands were beginning to throb. Scotty had Alice warming up on the third-base line. I knew I should try to stay in, even though my pitching was getting erratic. What if Alice blew up? That would mean Teri would have to pitch, and Ridgedale had some hot batters. Two women on and a home run would tie the score. I kept pitching.

"Niki," Scotty said when we went back into the dugout. "How are your hands? You're getting a little wild."

"They hurt," I said. "I was thinking, maybe if I pitch half the next? Then Alice could pitch an inning and a half. She could go in after the second out."

Scotty laughed. "Niki Etchen and her friend ego. Go and sit on the grass. You're through for the day. We'll do fine."

She was right, of course. Alice came in fresh and pitched beautifully. Not only that, but she hit a double. Not all pitchers are klutzes when it comes to swinging a bat. She did almost get beaned. Julie Baxter hurled her bat at her when she was struck out for the third and final time. Final because Julie was immediately tossed out of the game. We ended up winning 7–3.

The locker room was pandemonium, people screaming, snapping towels, and chattering about the Vallejo playoff games. But I was a little depressed, and I couldn't figure out why. Somehow I couldn't quite get into the spirit, now that it was over. Ginny invited everybody to her house for a beer bust. Don't hang around in drinking situations for a while, Mandy had counseled. I begged off. I wanted to go, but I figured it'd be too dangerous. I walked out feeling sorry for myself.

My parents chose that evening to call me into the living room for a "little talk." Ever since I overheard their late night conversation, I'd been formulating battle plans for the great revelation. The time never seemed right. It wasn't right now, but it appeared I'd been outflanked.

"We don't understand what's happening with you, Niki," Carl said. "First you quit the team, and then you run off to Carmel, then you rejoin the team and *win*—"

My mother cut into the happy look Carl started to get on his face when he remembered we'd won the division championship. "Never mind the team! The worst thing, Carl, is she ignores us!" My mother rounded on me, and I was startled to see tears bulging in her eyes. "Ever since you came back, you hide in your room for hours every night. You told me you'd talk—"

"Niki," my father asked seriously, "are you angry at us?"

"No!" I howled. I couldn't stand them being so worried and my mother crying and yelling at me.

"Are you sure?"

"Of course I'm sure!"

My mother lowered the boom. "Then why are you so angry right now?"

A flash flood of hopelessness and rage drowned out all the warning signals my head had been semaphoring since the "little talk" began. "I'm not angry at all at you!" I shouted. The only time I can be with you is cocktail hour! I've joined Alcoholics Anonymous, and it's too hard right now to be around drinking. That goes away in a little while," I added, hoping to soften the blow.

I could not have exploded a bigger bomb than if I'd told them I'd aborted myself and flushed the fetus down the toilet. The shock on their faces was straight out of the Sunday comics. I kept talking to try to bring some comprehension to those dead eyes. "See, I went down to Carmel so I could figure stuff out. Now that I know, all I have to do is not drink—"

"But surely—" my mother garbled. She stopped and looked at Carl. I wasn't going to get any help from her. Why hadn't I realized her worrying about my drinking too much was an entirely different matter from my insisting I was an alcoholic? Her sense of proprieties eliminated the worry. It was one thing having a teenager who lived in the fast lane; that could be "fixed" with time and understanding. Alcoholism was irreversible.

"You're going to college next year. When you're a senior," Carl said.

"You've been on the honor roll since junior high."

"You're a star athlete."

"And you have lots of good friends. How could you possibly imagine you're an alcoholic?"

There's nothing worse than having your own objections repeated back at you. "Lots of alcoholics are successful. It's a disease, and it can be arrested at any point. You don't have to fall all the way to Skid Row."

"A disease!" my mother shouted. "And where did you contract this disease? Is it passed through the clear blue sky—Carl! Say something!"

"There's nothing anyone can say," I insisted, furious at her. I sensed my father's bewilderment. He honestly felt he had taught me to approach alcohol in a mature fashion, divested it of its air of mystery and "forbidden fruit." My mother, on the other hand, seemed deliberately obtuse. "It's a physical allergy," I explained wearily, "as if I was allergic to dog hair. Some people have it and some don't. Simple."

Far from simple. My mother conjured up various alcoholic-as-social-leper scenes: "What will you do when your husband's boss proposes a toast? Announce you're an alcoholic?" She was certain I had signed away all chance of marriage, career, children, life itself.

My father kept asking me if someone convinced me I was an alcoholic, someone possibly opposed to drinking in general? Was there some weird group hanging around he hadn't heard of? It was his summing up that finally ended our conversation. First he choked on a piece of cheese to distract us from my mother's current scene—the wedding toast—then he said in a gravelly voice, "I believe you're a little confused about all this, Niki. You're not making much sense."

I dove up off the couch and screamed at them, "I don't have to defend myself against you! It's my life!" I watched them glance at each other. This is our reasonable daughter who maintains she's not angry? I stormed into the TV room and slammed the door. My hands were shaking, so I crammed them into fists and rocked back and forth, staring at the rug dully.

About two hours later my father walked in hesitantly and sat down without looking at me. I could tell he'd been drinking. His face was gray and tired. "Niki," he said suddenly, "if

I've hurt you . . . I'm sorry. The wine at dinner, I thought—"

"No," I said quickly. "It *is* a physical thing. Maybe I found out about it earlier this way, but it would have been true whether I started drinking at fourteen or thirty-five. Lots of people in A.A. never drank until their thirties. They're still alcoholics."

"But do you seriously think you are? How can you be sure? I've always trusted your judgment . . ." The ends of his sentences kept wisping off as he wrung his hands together.

"I'm sure," I said. I was so close to Carmel, to the screaming, to the terror on Martha's face.

"I've tried to let you make your own decisions because I knew you were capable of deciding well." He stopped and pressed his arms against his knees, as if he were pulling himself inside to marshal all his strength. "We'll change things around here," he said abruptly and walked out.

I noticed the first change when I got home the next day. The refrigerator was stocked with fruit juices and sodas. When we sat down for dinner, I got the message that was going to be the only alteration in our life-style. No one mentioned the "little talk"; my parents quaffed their wine and nattered on about political rebellions in South America. They had evidently talked it over in the cool light of day, decided I was nuts, but they'd humor me to the extent of ignoring my glass of milk. Their attitude was fine with me. I was already spending far too much time trying to assimilate my new identity as an alcoholic.

Sobriety was no joy, and it got worse day after day. I wasn't diving headfirst out of cars or waking up to crazy notes in the typewriter, but thinking I was an alcoholic was becoming an obsession in itself. Here is the alcoholic oiling her glove. Here is the alcoholic foolishly looking at the liquor store display window. It reminded me of when I started drinking heavier on the days I could, when Scotty had her system going. I'd never noticed every single bar and liquor store I drove past before. The meetings didn't help. Every time I walked into a Fellowship, I imagined I was a convict attending her mandatory sessions with the prison shrink. At least the convict had a chance to get paroled at the end of it. For me there was no end.

One thing I couldn't understand was the way the A.A. people yucked it up at the meetings. Some woman with ten years' sobriety would be chattering and knitting an afghan, looking as if she'd completed a series of deep-breathing exercises while she waited for the Seconal to hit. I was snappish and sullen, trying to free myself from the strait jacket so I could climb up the nearest wall. The A.A. members said my irritability was normal, that it would go away in a few weeks. I wasn't so sure. I didn't like being so nervous, and Martha and my parents didn't appreciate it much either. After Week One, I felt even more isolated than when I was drinking.

Since I couldn't seem to talk to Martha without blowing up at her, I spent all my free time at the meetings. I discovered a lot of people had been jailed and hospitalized when they were drinking. At first I was thankful that hadn't happened to me, but after a while I began to think I might have been too hasty in making a decision that was going to affect me forever. Did I really want to go through life as an alcoholic? It *was* my whole life, according to them. Being a little alcoholic, they said, is like being a little pregnant. The disease is incurable. They had a trick to get around the realization you could never drink again. Everyone was supposed to live in twenty-four-hour allotments, one day at a time. That way you wouldn't notice you'd committed yourself to a lifetime proposition. I ignored all that stuff, because I refused to run stupid games on my mind. If I decide I'm an alcoholic, I pledged to myself, I'll stop drinking for good. It was funny. One part of me would listen to the people's stories and say, Sure you're an alcoholic. Another part was analyzing and comparing. No, you're not, it would tell me. You didn't go to jail or wreck the car. Anyway, you're only seventeen. You're too young to die!

School somehow ground to an anticlimactic halt through all this. I was relieved. The only two things that were relevant to me at the moment were softball and whether I was an alcoholic.

Luckily, when I really needed a lift, I got my acceptance from the university. I ran right over to Martha's. "Look!" I screamed. "I got in! I'm in! I can take up to twelve units! That's a normal load, isn't it?"

"Yeah. That's neat, Niki. What classes are you going to take?"

"I don't know. Do you have a catalog?"

"I figured I'd get one later, when the class schedules come out."

"But they don't come out till September. Don't you want to decide now?"

Martha stretched her hurt leg and pounded at the muscle. "I hadn't really thought about it," she said.

"God, Martha, how can you be so lackadaisical? Our future stands before us! We're college students! Bluebooks! Midterms! We can smoke in class! C'mon, we have to go up there right this minute and get a catalog."

"I want to finish reading this book."

"Martha, how can you think of reading some stupid book when you are now a student of the greatest university system in the Western World? C'mon!"

"Jeez, Niki, we have all summer!"

"But we can decide what we're going to take and get last term's reading list and have a head start on everybody else!"

"Oh, Niki," Martha said disgustedly, but she trailed me out

the door, and by the time we'd parked and arrived at the student bookstore, she was almost as excited as I was. We found a hofbrau, got coffee, and sat down to investigate the catalog.

I was so up I couldn't believe it. Freedom! I never had to have lunch at high school again! Nobody took roll at college. Going to classes was at your own discretion. It made me twice as determined to do well. I wouldn't miss a single class, and I'd study, actually study, every single night! "Look," I said, "how about botany? That'd be interesting."

"Are you kidding? Stamens and pistils? I had enough of that in high school. No, look at this, Economic Theory I A. I like that."

"Yuck! The gold standard and the Federal Reserve Bank?"

"Hmmm. What about psych?"

"It all depends," I said importantly, "on whether it's experimental psych or not."

"Hi, Niki."

I swiveled around in my chair to face Mandy. I was startled for a minute, as if she didn't exist outside of A.A. A second later I recovered myself and motioned her to sit down. But I was irritated. Here I'm finally feeling good and Mandy has to come by and remind me. "Martha, this is Mandy. She's in A.A."

"Hi, Mandy."

I tried to think of a conversation that would interest them both. "Uh, Mandy, Martha is the one I told you about that first meeting. That I beat up?"

"Oh, right. You don't look permanently damaged."

"No," Martha said. "Teri kept telling me that alcoholics have to reach a crisis. I'm sorry the focal point of the crisis was my face, but it sure is nice Niki's not drinking."

"How long's it been, Niki?" Mandy asked.

"About two weeks, no big deal."

"Proabably the first time you haven't drunk in two weeks since you were thirteen," Martha said. "I'd call that a big deal."

"Fourteen, Martha. I started drinking at fourteen. Anyway, Mandy, we're up here checking out the courses in the catalog. I just got my acceptance, and Martha's starting in the fall too."

"I thought you were still in high school."

"I am, but I don't have any required courses left but civics, and I can fulfill that by taking one of the poli sci courses here. I can get in a full year of college my senior year."

"What's the big hurry?" Mandy asked. "God, Niki, lots of people in A.A. take off from whatever they're doing for their first year. You know, all those slogans—First things first; Easy does it. You should be concerned about your sobriety, not sneaking in an extra year of college."

Silence. It knocked the pins out of me. I didn't know what to answer. Martha sipped at her coffee. I was aware of her watching me. "I can handle it," I said finally. "I'm not going to sacrifice anything I want to do because of this drinking business. My life comes first. Anyway, what would be the point if I lay around doing nothing?"

"I didn't say do nothing," Mandy said. "For an alcoholic to stop drinking is a big job in itself. I meant not putting on extra pressure. If you have an easy senior year, you could get more involved in A.A. and do a lot of growing."

Growing! I thought disgustedly. I'm grown, lady, whether you can see it or not. This conversation was getting embarrassing in front of Martha. I wanted to cut it off. "School's no big pressure for me. It never has been."

Mandy shrugged and stood up to leave. "You coming to the meeting tonight?"

"No, I don't think so. We have games tomorrow and Sunday, and I have to rest up." The real reason was I didn't want

134

to shake my self-confidence dragging myself to a meeting and dwelling on the fact that I was an alcoholic. Screw it!

"O.K.," Mandy said. "Good luck. Nice meeting you, Martha."

The waiter took our empty cups and we sat there at the table, our mood of excitement snapped. I felt like a societal reject again, as if Mandy had suggested I was so sick I ought to commit myself for a year of seclusion. Forget her! Here I am, accepted a year early to college, about to go to the conference playoffs. I've been handling all that and more! I'm all right. Nobody's telling me I'm too untogether to take on any responsibility.

Martha lit a cigarette and idly thumbed through the catalog. "We might as well go," she said.

"Buncha bull," I muttered. "I'm not changing my plans, that's for sure. She talks like I'm some lousy invalid or—"

"I thought she was nice," Martha cut in. "She doesn't want you getting involved in a million different heavy things when—"

"She was mothering me," I snapped. "And so are you. So cool it. I'll make my own decisions. It's my life, right?"

"Yeah, it's your life," Martha said quietly. "But you didn't have any objection to being mothered or helped or whatever you want to call it when you were lying screaming on that bathroom floor in Carmel. All she was trying to say—"

"Shut up!" I yelled. I jumped up and hurled the catalog at her. People were staring at us. "Find your own way home," I snarled. I left her sitting there.

But after I'd gotten the car out of the parking garage, my anger drained away, and I felt guilty. I prowled by the bus stop, leaned over, and opened the car door. "Martha! Hey!" She looked at me, but she didn't come any closer. "Hey, Martha, I'm sorry. Come on."

She blew out a big stream of smoke and got in the car. We drove silently for a few miles. When we were getting near her place, I said, "Listen, all these people in A.A. say you get irritable for a while when you quit drinking. It's some chemical thing. I guess that must be it. I'm sorry."

Martha tapped the catalog on her knee. "O.K.," she said. "How long's this chemical thing supposed to last? You've been a real maniac lately."

"I don't know. Two or three weeks, I guess."

"Then it's almost over. I was afraid this was your new sober personality. I couldn't decide which was worse. You taking me and Teri up to Vallejo?"

"Yeah. We have to leave at eight."

"O.K., get some sleep."

I drove home, ticked off. I couldn't decide which was worse either. It was a bummer being so quick to anger. It seemed to me I was much nicer when I was drinking.

CHAPTER XVI

There were two games Saturday, two Sunday, five different teams. I looked at the schedule while we were checking into the hotel. "Unbelievable!" I shouted. "Did you see we get the dump spot? We don't play at all today, and we play twice tomorrow, at nine and at three."

"My fault," Scotty said. "I never was good at cards."

"Cards?" I said. "Cards!"

"Yeah, we cut the deck. I got a three. Not too hot, eh?"

"Jesus Christ! Cards! Our future rests on how you cut a deck of cards!"

"It's all chemical," Martha explained to a mystified audience as she dragged me over by a potted plant. "Calm down. We get four hours to rest, we only have to get psyched once, and we can spend today checking out the other teams. We'll know all about them."

"I suppose," I said. "There's nothing we can do about it anyway. But that means I have to pitch two games in a row."

"Alice can pitch most of one," Martha said. "Let's go out to the field."

"Practice at six-thirty," Scotty called. "When it's cooled

down. And tomorrow we play the two losers. Their morale will be down."

"Or way up," Teri said morosely.

It was clear right off that the West Bay team was the hot group. They whipped right through Tunnel. The North Bay–Central game was a little weird. North Bay was ahead from the first, but the Central dugout managed to goad their people into eking out a couple more runs. North Bay lost by one. I wasn't worried by Tunnel, but I figured North Bay had lost by a fluke. They were better than they'd shown today. Maybe they were nervous.

The hotel was jumping at night. Somebody from the West Bay team had bought a whole mess of beer, and the Central and West Bay teams spent all night screaming and yelling and carrying on. I was pissed, first because I couldn't drink and second because they were keeping me awake.

By Sunday I was in a horrible mood. "Look, Scotty," I said. "I think we should start off with me in the Tunnel game. Let Alice take over in the last two innings, and then start the North Bay game. I'll come in in the third. I'm worried about North Bay."

"Niki, keep your shirt on. I've been a coach awhile, and I can see which way the wind's blowing. Anyway, don't worry. We can lose one of these and still be in the competition. The only way we can blow it is to lose both."

I sighed. "All right, do it your own way." I stormed off to the room and got my glove and shoes. Martha was lying around reading a magazine. "How can you just lie there?" I yelled. "The conference playoffs, and you're reading?"

"You better relax," Martha said. "You're going to have a heart attack sitting on the bench."

"What do you mean, sitting on the bench?"

"If I were Scotty, I'd have Alice pitch the first game, and

you pitch against North Bay. That's the sensible way of doing it."

Which was exactly what Scotty did. I stormed around the dugout the whole first game, watching everything frantically. I was so nervous I could hardly see straight. When we beat Tunnel by two runs, I collapsed on the bench. "You see," Martha said. "You wore yourself out having a fit. There are sixteen people on this club. You don't have to supervise every little operation. Anyway, now we're in the slot. If we beat North Bay, that just narrows it down to three teams instead of four. Big deal."

I was furious. "Since we're in the slot, we might as well not even play North Bay, Martha. We know we're coming back next weekend. Is that your theory?"

"You're angry because you didn't have anything to do with us winning the slot. An individual—"

"Oh, shut up! You sound like Scotty."

"God, you make me so furious! I'd like to strangle you."

"You keep on saying that. Why don't you try it sometime and—"

"Stop it!" Scotty shouted. "I don't want to hear any arguments. We won our place. Everybody should be happy, not screaming at each other. How's your leg, Martha?"

"It's a lot better."

"All right, I want you to play the last two innings of this game with North Bay. Niki, since you're so hot to trot, why don't you pitch some to Martha and give her a little batting practice? And try to throw the ball across the plate, not at her head."

"O.K., O.K.," I said. I called Grace, the backup catcher, and we hustled out on the field.

"Now pitch 'em fast, Niki," Martha directed. "That North Bay pitcher is good."

I threw a couple of high outside pitches, but Martha wasn't fooled. When I tossed in my sinker, she slammed it clear across center field. It disappeared in some bushes near the fence. One of the sophomores went and got it. I tossed in some fast ones, and Martha hit a couple more, one a clear base hit unless their shortstop could jump nine feet, and another was a long fly to left. Then she peppered a few into right. "Come on, Niki," she called. "Throw me some hard ones."

"I am, Martha, I am. I'm glad you're on our team, not theirs."

We fooled around for ten more minutes, but I was getting discouraged. She slammed everything in the strike zone. "That's enough," I said. I waved off the fielders. "You don't need any more practice."

"This is far out," Martha bubbled. "Seems like I got better. Maybe by cooling it for a while I dropped all my bad habits."

I grinned. "Maybe. But you didn't do my confidence any good."

"You'll do great," Martha said, clapping me on the shoulder. "I know your pitching, that's all. Come on, let's go back to the hotel and rest."

My feet up in the air, a lemonade balanced on my stomach, I was thinking about this bad habit business. Since I'd stopped drinking for a bit, the blackouts might have gone away. Maybe I could drink O.K. again. You needed a rest, I told myself. You're not an alcoholic. Only I wasn't sure. I wished there were some blood test they could do and say if you were or you weren't.

The game was tense right from the start. North Bay was determined to win back their slot, and we'd already gotten ours, so maybe that was the difference. They had a little more hustle. By the third inning, we were down, 3–1. "Come on," I urged in the dugout. "Let's eliminate these people right now. Then we won't have to bother with them later."

Teri went out and hit a line drive. She was so tired she seemed to run at half speed to first. All the tension had gotten to everybody. She stepped off the base before the ball left the pitcher's hand, and we had one out. She came back to the dugout shaking her head. "What a dumb thing to do! I can't believe it!"

"It's all right," I said. But I was depressed when I went back out on the mound. Another inning, no runs. I had trouble with the first batter. We went up to a full count before I left her swinging. The next two popped up, and we were back in business. And back out of business right away. North Bay's pitcher was fast. She had less control than I did, but she really slammed the ball in. I didn't see how their catcher even held on to it. "I knew these people were good," I said miserably. "They were just messing around yesterday."

Scotty took out most of the first string and told them to go back to the hotel if they wanted. Nobody left. "I want to stay in," Teri said.

"No," Scotty said. "You're out. You're exhausted. This is a game, not a war."

I was disgusted. How did she expect us to win if she took out all our best players? The fielding fell apart, and they started racking up runs. Grace kept dropping the ball on the third strike, and I was getting really mad. "Grace, for God's sakes! That's the second out we should have had, and you let it get away! Stop dreaming!"

One batter after that, somebody hit a pop-up near the second-base bag. The shortstop and second baseman ran into each other, and the ball dropped right between them. I threw down my glove. "What the fuck is the matter with you guys? Come on!"

Scotty ran out on the field, her face furious. But instead of yelling at them, she came right up on the mound. "Now you listen to me, Niki. We've won our slot. I'm substituting in people who don't get to play all that much. Your screaming isn't helping anybody's confidence."

"But this fielding is—"

"Shut up! If you can't get with the right attitude, you can go back to the hotel. And clean up your language. The ump's going to toss you right off this field. If she doesn't, I will."

I started to answer back, but then I thought better of it. She was really angry. "All right," I said. I turned back to the batter.

The umpire said, for good measure I suppose, "Hey, pitcher! If you can't talk without swearing, maybe you better keep your mouth shut."

I did. We finally got out of the inning, 8–2. Martha came in that trip, but she couldn't hit for the whole team. They beat us, 10–4.

Martha, for once, was as angry as I was. "I can't believe Scotty would substitute in all those lame-ass people," she fumed on the way back. "Jesus! We could have dumped those creeps! All we accomplished was getting rid of Tunnel. We still have a four-team final."

"So what?" Teri said. "Anyway, you and Niki came in fresh. You can't expect Sarah to crouch out there hour after hour. And I'm exhausted. It's over. Let's forget it. We'll get 'em next weekend."

"Or they'll get us," I said bitterly. "West Bay. Did you see them?"

"They're the ones to beat, all right. If we ever get a chance to play 'em." Martha lit a cigarette and scowled out the window.

"You two are a real pleasure to be with," Teri said. "Think

142

I'll go to a meeting tonight. There's an Al-Anon half an hour later than the A.A., down at the Trinity Fellowship. Either of you want to come?"

"Not me," I said. "I'm staying home to sulk."

"I'll go," Martha said. "It might put me in a better mood. We have time to make it."

I dropped them off at Trinity. They both tried to convince me to come with them. "You can go to our meeting, Niki. People from A.A. come occasionally."

"No, I'm tired. How're you getting home?"

"We'll get a ride," Teri said. "Mandy and Frankie usually go to the A.A. meeting tonight."

"Good," Martha said. "Mandy seems nice. Maybe we can go out for coffee afterwards."

They went off chattering happily. I was lonely, jealous, and furious all at once. I slammed away from the curb, went home, told my parents about the games, and then twiddled my thumbs until they went to bed. The moment their door closed, I mixed myself a strong gin and tonic and parked myself in front of the tube, the volume tuned way low. Only I was too tired to even get drunk. I barely managed to sip half the drink before I dumped the rest down the sink and crawled off to bed.

Chapter XVII

The next day, I woke up groggy but pretty pleased with myself. Half a drink and I stopped. No problem, no desire for more. Martha was right about this bad habit business. All I needed was a little vacation from booze.

That night, testing out my new theory, it took me half a novel to sip through the contents of a rum and Coke. I woke up feeling fantastic. Far out! A piece of cake. I was enormously relieved to discover I wasn't an alcoholic. Three more nights, I decided, and I'll tell my parents the A.A. excursion was a big mistake.

I went to practice, pitched well, and even batted all right. When I got home, I remembered it was my parents' bridge night. Better all the time. I could actually drink my drink in the living room like a human being. I took a shower, popped open a beer, and couldn't stop. I got bombed.

When I stumbled into the kitchen the next morning, my father looked at me closely and asked if I was ill. "Maybe a little virus," I answered quickly. Ever since I'd come back from Carmel, they'd been treating me like the lab rat that's going to provide the cure for cancer. Just watch her closely, folks. The closer you watch, the faster you'll save ten thousand lives! God, why had I ever stopped drinking? And worse, why had I started again? At least I knew by his question I hadn't been falling over my feet when they got home from their bridge game. I tried frantically to dredge up some memory of going to bed, some little thing like taking off my shirt. But it was as if it had never happened. I mooned around the house, knowing all I needed was sleep, but I was too shaky and upset. Then Mandy called. I figured she wanted to hassle me about not going to the meetings.

"Hey, Niki," she said, "do you remember calling me last night?"

A big piece of ice shot into my stomach, and I couldn't say anything for a minute. "I called you?" I croaked.

"I figured you were blacked out, since you were so incoherent. I could hardly understand you."

"What did, uh, what did I want?"

"Who knows?" Mandy laughed. "You told me A.A. was a bunch of trash and injurious to one's self-esteem. You had trouble with that one. You had to repeat it about eight times before I had any idea what you were saying. Then you rambled on about losing the game, and how it was all your fault, that you were too irritable because you'd stopped drinking. Then you started crying and said you were lonely, and you couldn't stop drinking and you wanted to kill yourself."

"Oh," I mumbled.

"I told you when you sobered up to come to a meeting and you wouldn't be so lonely. But you said you couldn't get along with A.A. people, since you were basically such a louse. I told you a lot of alcoholics felt like louses when they were drunk, and all you had to do to feel better about yourself was to stay away from the first drink. You got angry and hung up."

"I—uh, sorry I bothered you," I finished stiffly. I felt like an incredible fool.

"That's all right, Niki. But call me sober next time. We might have a better talk. How do you feel?"

"Horrible," I said. "I don't know what to say. On Sunday and Monday I drank O.K. Then last night, I don't know, I didn't want to stop."

"One time when I was trying to convince myself I wasn't an alcoholic, I drank two beers a night for about three months. Then I went on a binge and ended up in the psych ward of General. That was when I was twenty. I drank for a year after that. Sometimes we're pretty stubborn. You want to go to a meeting tonight?"

"No, but thanks. I mean, thanks for understanding. It's uncomfortable at meetings. I feel all . . . separated."

"O.K., Niki. Come back or call me sober whenever you want."

I muttered a goodbye and sank down at the kitchen table. I wished even more there was some kind of blood test. One part of me kept saying, Look, stupid, obviously you're an alcoholic, accept it. And another part wouldn't do it. I stood up too quickly and had to grab at the edge of the table to keep from falling down. Damn! Why did this have to happen? I was doing so well. I went into my room and played solitaire, and finally I dragged out a bunch of A.A. pamphlets and started reading them. They made me feel a little better, and I was finally able to fall asleep.

When I got up again, I decided I might as well go to the meeting after all. I crept in ten minutes late and slumped down next to Mandy. She smiled at me and touched my hand. "The subject's guilt," she whispered.

I could say a lot about that, I thought. I'd never said any-

146

thing at a meeting before, not even that I was an alcoholic. When they called on me, I always passed. They were working around the room, and I started formulating what I wanted to say in my head. Most people said their feelings of guilt decreased immeasurably when they stopped drinking. "I accept myself the way I am," one man said. "I don't have to pretend I'm somebody else anymore. I like myself now. You only feel guilty when you think you're not living up to some standard you've set for yourself."

The woman leading the meeting called on Mandy. "I'm Mandy, and I'm an alcoholic," she said.

Everybody answered, "Hi, Mandy." It was a ritual they went through with each person. It set my teeth on edge.

"Guilt is egotistical," she said. "How could I, the great Mandy, have done anything so asinine? I love that definition of the alcoholic—an egotist with an inferiority complex. Of course, I get a lot of mileage out of feeling guilty; I can sit around and wallow in self-pity for days. It's a rest period. But then it occurred to me I could actually be happy and let myself rest too! I don't have to demand total commitment, total energy the moment I feel good. When I feel guilty now, I try to do something constructive. That gets me out of that self-pity, hate-myself bag. I could stew around in there forever, if I let myself."

She was talking to the whole meeting, but I felt she was directing her speech at me. An egotist with an inferiority complex? It sounded awfully familiar.

"Niki?" the woman said.

"I'm Niki, and I'm an alcoholic and—" I stopped talking while everybody said hi. My face was burning. Saying I was an alcoholic had knocked everything else out of my head. What was all that stuff I was going to say? "I pass."

"O.K. Frankie?"

147

I sat through the rest of the meeting berating myself. Why was I such a dunce? "My mind went blank," I said to Mandy after everybody had broken into groups for coffee.

"That's O.K.," she said. "I could hardly stammer out a word the first two months. No one cares."

Frankie handed me a cup of coffee and we all sat down.

"But I'm usually good at speaking in crowds," I said.

"This isn't exactly public speaking. It's a lot more personal."

"That's right," Frankie said. "If you're confused in your head, you're not going to give a lucid dissertation on the effects of guilt."

I smiled at her. "I still feel dumb."

"Hey," Mandy said. "You don't have to be a star ball player, first in your class, accelerated college student, *and* the best speaker in A.A. Give yourself a break."

"Anyway," Frankie added, "no one's into comparisons of what people say. It's a selfish program. Everybody's here to save their own ass. Whatever makes you comfortable, do it."

But what if that's drinking, I thought. *Does* drinking make me comfortable? Why do I keep vacillating back and forth? "It's all confusing," I said. "You're right that I'm concerned with this superficial best-at-this, great-at-that stuff. I must be insecure."

"No wonder," Frankie said. "When you're blacking out and hung over, and your life is a big haze you stumble through, you're bound to hang on to a few things for life preservers. For a long time I went around reminding myself I'd had a story published. That meant I was O.K., even though my life was this complete disaster. I don't have to do that anymore. I feel good about myself without the stories."

"I didn't know you wrote," I said. "I'd like to read some of your stuff."

I was happy by the time I left them. I'd been honest for

once and actually learned something about myself. If that's what Mandy meant by growing, that'd be O.K. I figured. I was too close to myself to have any perspective. Both Mandy and Frankie were students at the university. Frankie wrote. And they were both alcoholics. This A.A. stuff might not be so bad after all. I chatted reasonably with my parents and then fell into a peaceful sleep.

Chapter XVIII

One undeniable advantage of sobriety was waking up without a hangover. I bounded out of bed and ate a huge breakfast with Carl and Joyce. I was in such a good mood they got caught up in my excitement. By the end of breakfast, we'd planned a shopping expedition for a college wardrobe, a night at the symphony for my mother's birthday, and a Giants game for me and Carl. It occurred to me that the changes Carl had promised the night of our talk might come about—not the concrete alterations I'd expected at the time, but instead a gradual thawing of the distance between us as my own disposition brightened. A person obsessed with guilt and self-hatred doesn't make a happy companion.

I arrived at practice so high I felt I could skate across the clouds. Scotty began by calling a meeting on the grass. "For once I cut the cards right," she announced. "North Bay plays West Bay on Saturday, and we play Central." Everybody cheered.

"What a relief!" I said to Martha. "They'll be a cinch."

"Now," Scotty continued. "I don't want anyone sloughing off because they think Central is a crummy team. We're a lot better, but if we go into the game with the wrong attitude, they're going to beat us the same way they beat North Bay. A run here, a run there. They don't let down. They keep on plugging, and that's what we're going to have to do if we want to beat them. All right, infield practice. Barbara, take the outfielders over there and hit some flies to them. Alice, go over to the other diamond with the second string and play work-up, but you do all the pitching."

It was a long practice. Scotty peppered balls to us forever, and I pitched to everybody for batting practice. My high gave way to physical exhaustion. "God," I said to Martha, "I hope I recover by Saturday."

"She's a slave driver. Your hands are fine now, aren't they?"

"They were O.K. last week. How's your leg?"

"It's a lot better. I've been jogging in the evening after it cools off. You still look as if you've been through the wars, though."

I immediately flashed on my drinking. I stared at her. "Your nose, I mean," Martha said uncertainly.

I remembered Carmel. I have to be honest if I want to live. "I got drunk Tuesday night. I thought you knew somehow."

Martha shook her head. "No, I didn't know. You didn't have to tell me."

"I just wanted to. I felt bad, but I went to a meeting last night, and talked to Mandy and Frankie. It's O.K. now."

"Good. Don't hassle yourself about something that's over and done with. Come on, let's go home."

"Not the ice cream parlor?" I teased.

"Hmmm. Definitely the ice cream parlor."

In the middle of a double scoop of coffee fudge, Martha asked, "You seen Chuck lately?"

I halted mid-bite. "Chuck? Why would I see him?"

Martha shrugged. "Just wondering."

I drove home the long way. Martha's not-so-innocent question had planted the seed of an idea in my mind. If drinking had been the cause of my breakup with Chuck, and I wasn't drinking, why couldn't things go back the way they were? But *had* my drinking been the problem? Honesty, I commanded. I looked back on the final scene at the bar with fuller vision.

A friend of Martha's older brother Greg promised to get us in the bar on New Year's Eve. I was ecstatic. I'd never been in a real bar, not to drink at least. Chuck didn't want to go, especially when Martha and her date begged off. He had made some friends at the university who were having a big party at their fraternity. Frank at school was giving another party, the one Martha was going to. "Why can't we be with our friends?" Chuck complained. "It'll just be a bunch of strangers at the bar."

"We can hang out with our dumb friends anytime," I said. "I'm not giving up a chance to go to a bar. If you want to go to the parties, fine."

He ended up coming, as I'd known he would. He wasn't going to let his girl be alone on New Year's Eve. He didn't come along pleasantly, though. "We'll spend an hour or so here and then go to the frat house."

"Fine," I said equitably. I was willing to say anything. I could always change my mind later.

Three hours into the evening, he was ticked off. "Come on, Niki," he insisted. "Let's get out of here. We don't know anybody. It's a bore."

I was having a great time. So far I had ordered about eight different kinds of drinks and danced with a guy who said he was a truckdriver. This was what adults did when they·went out. "What can't we do here we can do at your fraternity?" I asked scornfully.

He glowered. "That oughta be obvious."

So he wanted to make out. I toyed with the idea a minute, but then dropped it. It was funny about stuff like that. If I was making out with Chuck, I was really into it. I couldn't think about anything else. But if I was drinking, I didn't want to make out. It was too distracting. I wanted to get drunk. "Forget it," I told him. "Look, stop being so sullen. Why don't you put on one of those hats, blow your horn, have some fun."

"Bull," he said. He slumped down in his chair. He wouldn't kiss me at midnight. When he took me home, he left the motor running. "Goodbye," I said, knowing it was the last time I'd see him.

"So long," he said, slamming the car into gear.

I barely had time to close the door before he roared off.

Martha was enraged. "What do you mean, you just said goodbye?"

"That's exactly what happened. We said goodbye, he drove off, and that's that."

"I don't get it. Didn't you talk or argue or scream or cry?"

I shrugged. "There was nothing to talk about. It just hit both of us at the same time we didn't get along."

"I don't know, Niki. You got along an awfully long time to suddenly decide you didn't get along."

It *was* a long time, I thought now. One and a half years of being together constantly. I decided it hadn't all been due to my drinking. A lot was Chuck's gnawing need for security and reassurance. I hadn't been able to give him what he craved then, and I wasn't sure I could do it now, or even wanted to. His criticisms about my athletics and newspaper work had hurt more than I'd realized. If his method of demanding attention was to downplay my accomplishments, I wouldn't wish myself back in that situation, drunk or sober. On the other hand, his carping could have been pent-up resentment over

153

my desire to be alone occasionally. If I hadn't been drinking, I might have had more to give him during the times we *were* together.

I pulled up in front of our house and sat in the car, staring at the Rosefelds' big elm next door. It's been over for six months, I told myself. But I couldn't help wondering how he'd react if I told him I'd stopped drinking.

Sarah drove up with us to Vallejo on Saturday, and on the way she relayed the gossip about West Bay. "Their catcher and right fielder had these big vacations planned," she said, "and they canceled them because they're so sure they'll win and go on to the state championships."

"Too bad for them," Teri said. "All those plans blown for nothing."

"Don't be so sure," Martha said. "We have to beat Central first."

"Besides," I added, "maybe North Bay will beat West Bay and we'll end up playing them again."

"No way," Teri said positively. "It's going to be us against West Bay."

That was the way it happened, only there was a little hassle first. We beat Central hands-down, Alice pitching the whole game. Scotty started out with the second string, and by the end of the game, half the second team was still playing. Central had been flying high and then bottomed out. Both Ridgedale and Washington had challenged us a lot more.

Then came the game between North and West Bay. A lot of our team went back to the hotel to celebrate, but a few of us stayed on to watch. It was a hostile, heavy game. Fielders ran into runners, the pitchers beaned a couple of people, everybody tried to get everybody else out on injuries. "This is terrible," Teri said. "This isn't sports."

I grimaced as they chalked another West Bay run on the

scoreboard. "I'm not too thrilled about playing these people."

"You and me both," Martha said. "If one of those bitches rams into my leg, it's had it. I'm scared."

North Bay lost by three runs, and the mood was ugly. Their shortstop saw us sitting in the stands and yelled, "Hey punks! They're gonna wipe up the field with you. It's not fair you play in the final. We whipped your asses."

"You got your chance," Sarah said mildly. "And you lost. So cool out."

"You tellin' me to cool out? Who'd you play to get in the final? Central and Tunnel. The two worst teams. They oughta make this a two-game-out-of-three series between us and them. You don't belong on the same field."

"You lost to Central," Ginny pointed out. "You got no complaints."

The shortstop was joined by a couple of fielders. "They're gonna rip your behinds, turkeys. And we'll be out here watching."

Teri said, "Come on, let's split," to all of us.

"Ah-ha!" Shortstop crowed. "They're scared. Didja see us running when they started plowing into *us?*"

"I don't think that's sports," Teri said stolidly.

"Oh! You don't think that's sports, huh? Let me tell you—" She started moving up the stands, her fielders at her rear.

"Hold on," Sarah said. "We've got no fight with you." She stood between them and us, and we all waited. At the first shove, we were ready. The bitterness and anger in the air made me spit a sour taste out of my mouth. Shortstop looked at me. In the silence, Teri said, "Let's go back to the hotel."

We started moving past them, walking by quietly, each of us still ready to whirl around and fight if anyone even made a gesture. None of us looked back when we were walking to the gate, but we knew they were watching. We crowded in the

155

car, and Sarah started crying, mostly out of relief. "Boy," she said, "that could have been horrible. Fighting in the bleachers? What are they so ticked off about?"

"They're furious they lost, that's all," Teri said. "We would have made the perfect punching bags. It was close."

We got back and separated to our rooms without talking. All of us felt a little down, as if we'd been cowardly. But if we'd fought, at least a couple of us would have been too hurt to play the next day. I kept trying to convince myself we had done the right thing.

"You must be mellowing out," Martha said after we'd collapsed on the beds. "I kept waiting for you to start something, and you kept your mouth shut."

I couldn't tell whether she was complimenting me or insulting me. I grunted, picked up an A.A. pamphlet, and started to read it. But it seemed unreal: Turn your life over to the care of God as you understand Him, and all that bull. The real world was out there, in confrontations like that. Did you wipe 'em out, or did you wait and bide your time? A.A. didn't help there. I finally fell asleep until the practice.

I don't know how she did it, but Scotty knew about the almost fight. "I want to thank the five of you," she said, "for showing the good sense to walk away instead of wading in. The last thing we need tomorrow is to have half our starting team in the hospital. Let's go."

The practice was short, and we had the whole night to kill. I was bored. I paced around the room, looking out the windows, examining the hotel stationery, anything. "Why don't you go to a meeting?" Martha suggested.

"Are you crazy? Drive all the way—"

"No! There are meetings all over. Call the A.A. number in the phone book and ask where. I'll go with you."

I thought about it for a minute. It might make me feel better. "No, that's stupid. I should be resting."

I lay down on the bed and told myself to rest. I tried to meditate, but my head kept intruding. How the hell *did* people meditate? I figured they were pretending. Finally I organized a little group to go to a movie. I had to do something. I was going crazy.

I woke up at six-thirty and went down to the dining room and ate breakfast. Martha was still asleep when I got back up to the room. I didn't see how Martha could be so calm. She sure was a lot different from me. I was about ready to crawl out of my skin.

I went outside the hotel and walked around. I wanted to talk to somebody. I was so nervous. There might be an A.A. meeting— At eight o'clock Sunday morning? Idiot! It worried me I couldn't calm myself down without thinking of A.A. You're getting trapped, kiddo, I said to myself. They're drawing you in their web. Pretty soon you'll think you can't move unless someone in A.A. says you can. I shivered. Maybe I could go to one meeting a month, to remind myself I was an alcoholic and couldn't drink. Then I wouldn't get seduced into all their weird games.

Martha was up when I got back, putting on her shoes. Her glove was sitting on the bed.

"All set?" I asked.

"The game doesn't start for an hour, but let's go out anyway. I'm nervous as hell."

Teri and Sarah were already there, tossing a ball back and forth. Martha and I joined them for a few minutes and then we all went to the dugout. "Do you think they'll be like they were yesterday?" Sarah asked.

"I don't know," we all mumbled at once.

Scotty stalked into the dugout. I could see the lines of strain around her eyes. Most of our team crowded after her. "Now look," she said, "I know this is asking a lot. But if they start shoving people the way they did with North Bay, I want you

157

to turn the other cheek. Don't try to get back at them. This is a sport, and that's it. Even if we lose, I want all of us to feel we gave our best and behaved decently. Does anybody want to say anything?"

"What if somebody gets hurt?" a sophomore said. "I mean badly."

"Then that's on them, not us. Two wrongs don't make a right."

"They'll come back as leprous rats in their next lifetimes," Sarah said to the sophomore. The laughter cut the tension, and Scotty began infield practice. Sarah and I went off by the dugout to warm up. When I looked out at the field again, I realized the stands were teeming with people. Some of the guys from the boys' team were there. I waved at Frank. He made a circle with his thumb and forefinger. It made me feel good they'd come, that we had some support from our school.

We were up first and back down again in about ten minutes. Their pitcher was good. She even struck Martha out. I went up to the mound and faced their first batter. She was a short, powerful-looking girl, and she hunched over so much the strike zone seemed no more than a foot high. "Come on, Niki," Sarah called. "Come on, baby, right in here, kid, come on—" I threw, and Sarah yelled, "Swing!"

The girl swung at a high outside pitch. She stepped out of the box, pointing at Sarah. "Tell her to quit doing that."

"What?" Sarah said innocently.

"Saying 'swing,' that's what!"

"No law against it," the umpire said. "You'll just have to keep your ears buttoned."

I grinned, and Sarah raised her eyebrows at me. I slammed in a fastball. The girl watched it go by, determined not to swing when Sarah yelled. "Strike two," the umpire bawled.

"O.K., Niki," Sarah called. "You're way ahead of her, kid,

come on, right in the mitt— Swing!" The batter swung on another high pitch and popped it up. She ran it, but Ginny didn't have to move an inch. She snatched it out of the air. "One down," everybody yelled behind me.

I struck the next batter out, and then lost one. She made a standing double. Their fourth-position batter flied out, and we were back at bat, nothing to nothing. Teri led off with a double. Barbara got a short single, not quite long enough to score Teri. When Barbara started to steal on a high pitch, the catcher threw down to second, and Teri, with long lead at third, ran for home and slid in under the return throw. "Safe!" the ump bawled. The stands blew up; I was surprised to see some of the North Bay people cheering. Apparently they'd decided we weren't their enemies after all. We had a time-out while the coach took their catcher aside and probably promised to murder her if she threw to second in that situation again. Then we were back on the field, two strike-outs and a pop-up.

Their fifth-position batter looked mean. I wound up, spun one over, and she smashed it hard, right at my head. I didn't even think about catching it; I hit the dirt. When I got to my feet, she was on second. Our center fielder had scooped it up on the run. "Whatsa matter, pitcher?" West Bay yelled from their dugout. "Things too rough out there for ya?"

I took the ump's advice and shut my ears to everything but Sarah's steady chatter. But I was shaken. I walked the next batter, and the seventh hit a stand-up double that scored the two on base. Sarah trotted out to the mound. "Freaked you out, eh?"

"Yeah."

She clapped her hand to my arm. "Look, I got a little tip on this number eight. She likes 'em high and inside. She never hits low balls. Keep 'em down and across the outside corner. And cheer up—this is only the second."

159

I sighed. Just another game. I settled in, pitched her straight across the knees one right after the other, and she went down looking. The pitcher struck out, and number one popped up again.

I was the lead-off batter. "Jeez," I said to Scotty, "I wish they'd get designated hitters in softball."

"Go on," Scotty said. "A walk's as good as a hit. Watch 'em close."

I stepped up to the plate, ground in my shoes, and the pitcher threw a fastball right at my head. I bailed out so fast I didn't know I'd done it till I found myself on the ground. When I got back up, my knees were shaking. Cool down, I said. Just cool down. The next was so inside I jumped on the plate and felt the ball whiz past my back. "Ball two!" The crowd was muttering behind me. I walked out of the box and did a couple of stretching motions.

"You got her going now," their catcher yelled. "You got her, baby!" I stepped back in the box and watched a strike float by. Another missed the corner. Then she lost me on a low ball. I flipped the bat to Sarah and jogged to first base. Teri was standing in the coaching box.

"What're you doing here?" I asked her.

"Alice had to piss," she said. "I can't believe it. Was she doing it on purpose?"

"That first one was on purpose. I'm not sure about the second. My stomach feels funny."

"All right. Listen to me and don't think about anything else."

The pitcher wound up, and the moment she let go of it, I scampered off the bag. Smack into the catcher's mitt, and I scrambled back. On the next pitch Sarah crouched, and I moved off fast, waiting for the hit. But she fanned it, and the catcher jumped up and threw to first. The first baseman was

160

napping. She missed the throw, and Teri screamed, "GO!" I pounded down the line, listening only for Teri's voice telling me to slide. All of a sudden, the second baseman crouched in front of the bag like a defensive lineman, and the ball hit me hard between the shoulder blades. I flipped over the baseman and landed on my back. There was that panic when I couldn't breathe. People were moving around me, and I instinctively pulled my hands in to protect them.

Then the air flooded back, and I heard the field umpire yelling, "Interference! Runner on second is safe!"

I got up and Teri grabbed my arm. We walked back and forth near the bag. "I'm O.K.," I said. Teri turned to the second baseman. "I'm going to knock your teeth down your throat you do that again."

"Big talk." The woman sneered.

"Just remember," Teri said. She trotted back up to the coach's box, and I felt denuded, stuck out in enemy territory.

But next pitch, Sarah hit a quick single, and Scotty stopped me at third. "Are you all right?"

I nodded, watching Martha step up to the plate. She smashed a stinging grounder, and I had a good lead. I crossed the plate and fell into the dugout thankfully. Sarah followed me in. "Forced out at second," she explained. "They took the easy out. But that lame-o on second slammed her elbow in my face when I ran in." She rubbed her jaw.

"She's a nice one," I said. I closed my eyes and pretended I was anywhere else but here.

Martha was picked off trying to steal second while Ginny was up. She collapsed next to me on the bench. "I can't run fast enough," she moaned. "This game is horrible."

I kept my eyes closed, thinking about a nice lake, but I opened them when the crowd started screaming. Ginny had hit a long, long ball, and Scotty was urging her into third.

"Stop!" she yelled, throwing up her hands. Ginny glanced over her shoulder and made the turn. She slid into home an instant ahead of the ball. "Don't *ever* do that again," Scotty shouted, but she was grinning, and the game suddenly got interesting again. Teri smacked a near base hit, stopped only by their shortstop's lunging catch. "I don't understand it," Scotty said. "They're good. They don't have to pull all this dirty stuff."

I went back out on the mound and threw a sinker the first batter popped up to Barbara. The second batter hit a grounder to Teri. She scooped it out of the dirt and threw to Martha. Easy out, I thought. Two down. But just as Martha straightened up from the catch, the runner stomped on her foot and shoved with her shoulder. Martha twisted around, and her cry of pain rocketed through me with such force I thought I was the one who had cried out. No one paid any attention as the runner pounded into second. I was on my knees at first base. Martha's face was dead-white, contorted with pain.

I heard Frank behind me. "What is this?" he shouted. "They brushback Niki, and smash Sarah and—"

"Who are you?" the ump shouted. "Get off this field!"

"But you can't—"

Martha was gripping my hand so hard I had to bite my lip. She was writhing around, her face getting grayer.

"I'm filing a protest," I heard Scotty say. "We're protesting this game. I'm not subjecting sixteen- and seventeen-year-old girls to this kind of play because the umpires aren't—"

"Martha," I mumbled. Then I swung around and shouted at them, "Forget the game! Do something about her!" But somebody was doing something, because Frank's old car ground to a halt in front of me, and Roger jumped out. He and Frank lifted Martha into the back seat, and I followed her in, still holding her hand. I propped her head in my lap, while I hollered at Teri and Sarah to meet us at the hospital. Roger handed me his jacket, and I tucked it around her while Frank wheeled his car out the park gate. I looked at street signs as we whipped by. I couldn't stand all the pain in her face.

Thank God it was an efficient hospital. A nurse saw us coming and ran for a cart. Frank and Roger lifted her on. "Her leg," I gasped. "Her right leg."

"All right," the nurse said. "Listen, honey, you have to let go of your friend's hand. It's all right now."

"Niki?" Martha mumbled.

"I'll be right out here. I won't leave for a second, honest." Her hand loosened, and the nurse wheeled her behind a closed door. I slumped down into a chair. I heard Roger giving information about Lincoln's athletic insurance to some official. I was suddenly desolate, and I started crying. Frank put his arm around my shoulders, and I sagged against him. "I can't believe it," I said.

"Neither can I. That was . . . I don't even know the word. Same leg?"

I nodded and breathed deeply a few times. It stopped the crying, but then I felt my stomach heaving and I had to bolt to the ladies' room. When I got back, Teri was talking to Frank and Roger. "Are you all right?" she asked me. I guess I looked pretty green.

"I threw up, but I'm O.K. now. Any word?"

"Not yet. You were only gone a few minutes." Frank lit a cigarette and handed it to me.

"Thanks," I mumbled.

Teri, who didn't smoke, accepted Frank's offer of a cigarette and puffed at it nervously. "Scotty marched the team off the field and told them she was filing a protest Monday morning against both the umpires and West Bay. The umps screamed and yelled, but she wouldn't listen. They said if we pulled out, we were conceding the game, and she told them to shove it."

"Is there any way we can find out what's going on?" I asked dully. Everybody looked blank. "With Martha, I mean."

"I'll ask," Roger said.

"Niki," Teri said. "I drove your car over, and I got yours and Martha's stuff."

"From the hotel?"

"Oh, no, I should have thought of that. Give me your room key. I'll pick up Sarah on the way. She stayed to help get the equipment together. I'll be back in twenty minutes."

Teri left and Scotty swept in. I was beginning to feel punchy. "How is she?" Scotty asked.

"Roger's trying to find out," I said.

Having ascertained that Martha was in limbo, Scotty launched into her attack. "Niki, I don't know what you thought you were doing, but let me tell you if you *ever* move an injured player again . . . You know you call for an ambulance. What if her leg had been broken?"

"It wasn't."

"You don't know that even now. Plus what the insurance company would say. And what the league will say."

"I don't care what anybody says."

"I don't care that you don't care, Niki. I'm tired of your prima-donna act. People function as a unit, not a bunch of half-assed individuals playing Superman. You apparently haven't learned—"

"Hey," Frank interrupted, "this isn't fair. Roger and I got the car, and we took—"

"Yeah, you two were a big help. 'Who was that kid?' the umpire kept asking."

"He was the only one doing anything," I flared. "You were

164

arguing about the game. No one was paying any attention to Martha! She could have died for all you cared!"

Roger came back in the sudden silence. "She's all right," he reported. "They shot some muscle relaxant into her leg, and they're taping it now. They also gave her some painkillers, and they said she'll be dopey when she comes out. But she's all right."

I put my hand in front of my face. I was starting to cry again with the sudden lessening of tension. I got up and walked away from the others. My insides felt like jelly. I couldn't take any more of Scotty's haranguing.

When Martha hobbled out on a crutch, I ran up to her. Her eyes were funny. "Oh, you've been crying," she said. "You shouldn't do that. See, we worry about each other too much. I'm all right."

She was slurring her words, and I laughed. "Boy, are you stoned! Teri got our stuff, and she's picking up Sarah—"

"Hi, Scotty," Martha said. "Did we win?"

"We stopped the game," Scotty explained.

"Because of me?" Martha said, amazed. "You shouldn't have done that. How will we ever know who won?"

"Scotty's filing a protest," I said. "Monday morning."

"But what will happen then?"

"Who knows?" I said irritably. I couldn't believe Martha was so upset about the outcome of the game. It must be because she's stoned. I heard Teri calling me from down the hall. "Come on," I said. "Teri's back with the car."

"I want Martha to come back on the team bus," Scotty said.

I looked at her. "No."

"I said—" Scotty repeated.

"And I said no. She's coming back with me. Come on, Martha."

Martha looked confused, but Teri ran up, unaware of the argument. She took Martha's arm. "Car's right outside," she said. "Lemme help you." The three of us moved off.

"Thanks, Frank, Roger," I called over my shoulder. Scotty stood there looking as if somebody had slammed her over the head with a brick.

I got in the back with Martha, and Teri drove. We said hardly anything on the way. Martha fell asleep, and I was too drained to open my mouth. Teri and Sarah must have felt the same way. Martha was groggy when we brought her into her house, and we had to explain everything to her parents and brother twice over. Then Teri drove to her house and hopped out, leaving the motor running. "I'd invite you in," she said, "but my father's off again, and Sunday is one of his big drinking days. I'll talk to you soon."

I switched to the driver's seat and thought, Poor Teri. What a drag to have to go home to that. And then I remembered. I couldn't believe it. I'd forgotten about myself for hours, for a lifetime. It was the first time I hadn't thought about the drinking thing since Carmel. Somebody had axed away my chains while I was asleep. What a relief!

When I got to Sarah's house to drop her off, she asked me to come in. "My parents went on a drive," she said. "I could use some company for a while." I didn't want to, but I couldn't say no. I followed her inside. "Boy!" she said. "I could use a beer. You want one?"

The idea staggered me for a second. A beer? A beer. Sarah looked at me strangely, and then remembered. "Oh, Niki. I forgot. I'm sorry. How 'bout a Coke?"

"No," I said. "A beer will be fine."

She hesitated. "Are you sure?"

"Sure I'm sure." She was a little baffled, but what could she say? She pulled two beers out of the refrigerator.

CHAPTER XIX

I spent most of the next few days at Martha's, playing Scrabble and reading out loud to her. We finally went through the catalog, and I decided what courses to take. Martha had a long list of possibilities. She said it was silly to decide so early. "After all, I might suddenly want to become a chemical engineer in September, right?"

"Highly unlikely," I said. I leaned back from the Scrabble board, having lost my third straight game. "I sure am glad that hospital was good. I would have had heart attacks if you'd just lain there waiting."

"What was all that stuff about going back on the bus? I meant to ask you, but I forgot."

"I don't know. Scotty wanted you to go on the bus, and I didn't."

"Have you talked to her yet?"

I shook my head. As far as I was concerned, Scotty could go hang herself.

"Boy, it was weird," Martha said. "I was so out-of-it. I barely remembered that conversation. I don't remember coming in the house when we got back. I sort of recall you and my mother talking and me in bed. And then nothing."

"You were pretty stoned, all right. Not making much sense."

"That's a switch. For once I was the one that couldn't talk. It made me feel icky later. Was I being a dope?"

I laughed. "Now you know what I go through every time I get drunk. No, you were fine."

"Is a blackout like that, where you don't remember anything?"

"Unh-huh. Exactly."

"Yuck. I wouldn't like that. You must be glad you're not drinking."

I got up and looked out the window. I didn't want to tell her, but I knew I had to. The world seemed like an enormous pawnshop. I had a pocketful of tickets, and the only way I could redeem myself was to pay off in explanations and apologies. "I *have* been drinking. Not drunk, though, just a little high. I guess I don't like A.A."

"Teri says there are other programs, Niki. You don't have to do A.A. She says—"

"But Martha, I don't want to stop drinking."

"Oh." That brought her up short, and I could almost hear the wheels whirling around in her head. "O.K.," she said finally.

I grinned. "You really had to force that out, Martha. The Al-Anon trip. I'd have to have the mentality of a chimpanzee not to see through you." I was still smiling, but my voice got harder.

Martha gazed up at the ceiling, ignoring my barely concealed anger. "It's hard for me to admit I can't do anything about your drinking. I don't appreciate how important it is to you. I thought I did, in Carmel, but it kind of faded away. I have these imaginary conversations where I say, Listen, Niki, I know how hard it is for you to see how drinking messes you up, 'cause you're still in the middle of it, but I'm your best friend, and I think you'd be happier if you stopped. You say, Yeah, you're right. And that would be the end of it. Only it doesn't work that way. If I sound patronizing, it's because I can't understand why I can't convince you you're an alcoholic instead of you convincing yourself. It's my problem."

I sat down on the bed and sighed. A million responses leapt into my head, but every one of them was defensive. Martha had been open. She wasn't attacking me. She honestly believed I was an alcoholic. I probably was an alcoholic. Or pre-alcoholic, I hedged. But I still didn't want to stop drinking.

"It's my life," I said apologetically. It sounded lame, but she smiled and nodded. "That's right. But Niki, I can't take another drunken scene like Carmel. I don't want to see you drunk. It's not you. It's somebody else that scares me. O.K.?"

She was trying desperately not to sound harsh. I could see the caring in her face. I reached out and took her hand. "O.K.," I said. "I understand. I won't drink around you."

"Thanks. You want to try another game?"

"God, no, it's too depressing. No fun when you know you don't have a chance of winning."

"I could shut one eye. Or take four tiles when you get seven."

"Martha the handicapper. Forget it. My pride would suffer. I'm going home for a while. I'll catch ya later."

I drove home wondering whether it would be a hassle not to drink around Martha. We hadn't set any time limit. I guess we could go to alternate parties or something. But what if I wanted her to come with me on a vacation? Or we went out to dinner? It would be a big drag if I could never go anywhere with her because she didn't want to see me drinking. Of course, I told myself, you could always not drink, just for that dinner or this party. But I knew I'd be irritable at Martha if I was with her and couldn't drink. So I might as well not be with her at all. Why was everything so complicated? But Martha had the right to set things up the way she wanted in terms of my drinking. It was a reasonable decision. I told myself that all the way home. And once I'd gotten there, I turned right around and went to the liquor store.

I bought a six-pack and went up to the park. I lazed around on the grass, drinking the beer, but I got lonely fast. It seemed I didn't have any drinking buddies anymore. I couldn't drink in front of Martha, and Teri and Sarah knew about my sojourn in A.A. None of them drank much anyway. It makes you feel weird when you're on your seventh beer and wanting to go to the store for more when everybody else stopped at beer number two. There was always Sam. But he made me uncomfortable, with his cute comments about my drinking, and the way he hassled me about sleeping with him. Besides, he had such a huge rep as the school drunk, our drinking together seemed a little like ending up on Skid Row.

I traced a pattern on a patch of dirt and opened up another beer. The trouble with booze, I thought, is it doesn't tell you how great you are, or smile at you, or hold your hand. It never even talks. "You're not very good company," I said to the beer in my hand. It didn't answer. It sat there fizzing, the way it was supposed to. "You do your trip, I'll do mine," I said to it. A man walking by looked at me oddly. I figured it was time to leave.

On the way home, I started thinking about Sam again. If I was going to be honest about it, at this point I had to admit the only thing separating our drinking was he drank during the day, and I drank at night, alone in my room. I realized I was being an idiot. What I needed was social drinking, socially acceptable everyday drinking, so I could forget this alcoholic stuff. The thing to do was join my parents again for cocktails and dinner. I'd be happy, they'd be happy, and everything would go back to normal, including me.

I didn't want to make a big announcement to them, so I wandered into the kitchen when my father was mixing drinks. "I'd like a gin and tonic tonight," I said.

He stopped playing with the swizzle stick and looked at me. "I thought you'd stopped drinking," he said.

"I did. But I'm giving up on that jazz. Those A.A. people are weird."

Giving up was definitely the wrong term to use. It awakened the fighter that lurked beneath my father's businessman facade. "What do you mean, giving up?" he demanded. "The way you gave up the team? Let's see, seems I remember hearing you're supposed to call someone in A.A. when you feel like giving up. Isn't that right?"

I blinked at him; this wasn't the way it was supposed to go at all. I'd expected him to welcome me back to the drinking fold with open arms. Instead he was calling Joyce into the kitchen for a "discussion."

"I realized I'm not an alcoholic," I said. "Why on earth would I call anyone? I was only going to A.A. to find out, anyway."

"That wasn't what you told me," Carl countered.

"Why did you think you were an alcoholic in the first place?" my mother wanted to know. "I don't see how you can expect us to make a judgment about your drinking if you can't—"

"What's to decide?" I asked irritably. My father was actually blocking the liquor cabinet as if I was going to dive in and snatch up the bottle of gin.

"What's to decide is you're a minor living under your parents' roof, that's what!" my father thundered. "You've put this whole family in an uproar over this alcoholism business, and now you expect us to ignore you ever said it. I want an explanation!"

Explanations again! "What do you want me to do," I yelled, "buy a half-hour on the local news and tell the whole Bay Area I made a mistake? I made a mistake, that's all."

We stared at each other, not knowing what to say. "Forget it," I snapped. "It's not worth it." I stormed into the TV room and flung myself on the daybed. Then I stormed back up and grabbed a beer out of the little bar refrigerator and sat there drinking it while I read some of my mother's new Book-of-the-Month selection. A half-hour later my father stuck his head in the door, noticed the beer, and announced dinner was ready. When I went to the table, a glass of milk sat next to my plate. That was the way they kept on, ignoring the few beers I drank in the TV room, but no more cocktails, no wine with dinner. There wasn't one place I could drink comfortably, all because I'd gotten hysterical and run off to A.A. before I was ready. I started doing a few babysitting gigs so I could replenish the bottles in the back of my closet.

The next two weeks were busy. We still practiced, since the outcome of the game hadn't been decided, and I took Martha to the doctor a few times to see about her leg. They thought at first they were going to have to operate. Martha refused point-blank to even step into the doctor's office if he continued pressing the idea. She said that all those operations did was leave a lot of scar tissue and rack up your legs worse. I privately agreed, but I counseled an open mind and an intelligent decision, so we discovered a lot about ligaments, joints, and muscles from the books I got out of the library. Martha seemed interested in the stuff we learned, but I could see she didn't think it related to her. All these calcium deposits and ripped ligaments were in other people's legs; her leg was filled with Martha and off limits to nosy doctors.

Then the summer crashed into its long, hideous dead self. I always hated the summer anyway, since heat bugs me. And it was *so* boring. I needed all that acclaim I got at school. I felt sort of lost without it. Last summer, I'd had a part-time job, but I hadn't looked for one this year because of softball. Now any idea we'd had of going to the state championships was blown too. Martha phoned to tell me one morning. "We're not supposed to know yet," she said. "Scotty's planning to tell us at practice. The decision's irrevocable."

"I don't understand. We were supposed to wait for the umps to do something?"

"Right. Decisions on the field are unarguable during a game. Each separate incident is decided. If the umps notice a lot of fishy things, then they themselves have to do something. The teams keep playing and protest afterwards. The field umpire said she was going to do something after my accident, but Scotty herded everybody off the field before she had a chance. The plate ump said sports are rough, and if you play, you gotta take it."

"Hmmm. So we supposedly conceded the game. How can you concede a game with a one-run lead?"

"I don't know. It's a pretty funny way to lose a conference championship."

I didn't go to the practice that day. Scotty and I were barely speaking, and I already knew the decision. It's funny, but I wasn't as disappointed as I thought I'd be. The violence of the last game, Scotty's continual haranguing, and Martha's injury combined to cancel out my enjoyment of softball. I wasn't sure we would even do well at the state championships. Teri had started her summer job. Paying for her college education was more important than a brief moment in the limelight. And Martha couldn't play. Their bats out of the lineup would seriously damage our chances.

The summer ground along, and my parents gradually let up a bit. We had champagne on my mother's birthday, and I had wine a few times when we went out to dinner. My father began to regale me with stuffy lectures about choosing one's major, and the necessity of specialization in our complex society. It seemed to be a process of slow readmittance to the family.

The day we trekked off in search of a fall wardrobe, we ended up going to a movie together for the first time in my memory. When we got home, my father opened a sparkling dessert wine, and I modeled my new clothes for them. But I was careful to confine my heavy drinking to my room, after they'd gone to bed. I didn't want to give them any reason to think they were forced to reopen the alcoholism issue. Luckily, they didn't want to talk about it any more than I did. I realized I had unwittingly cast aspersions on their drinking by questioning my own. They were as defensive with me as I was with them. Cocktail hour, wine tasting, visits to the pool hall could no longer be considered harmless family entertainments. So though they did let up, if only to make it more comfortable for themselves, life never went back to the way it had been before Carmel. Even with three-quarters of his attention diverted by a baseball game, Carl would say as I was pulling my fifth beer out of the bar refrigerator, "Hey, Niki, that's enough. You're not going to be able to fit into all those clothes you got for school."

In spite of my parents, I seemed to be drinking more. I was so bored! The only way of getting through the summer was to booze my way into September. I'd cool it when I started my university classes. Meanwhile I was trying a new policy of accepting myself. I would read the little notes in the typewriter, and I'd think, I have been depressed, so it's not strange I would write that. It kind of worked, but every once in a while I'd get this feeling that my life was a shaky house of cards, and each

174

new year added another card, unbalancing the whole mess all the more. Inevitably the card house was going to come crashing down.

One night, I drank a few beers, went back to my room, and just couldn't face that lonely gulping at the gin bottle. I needed people. I snuck out of the house and drove slowly to a pizza place. I was hidden in a corner drinking beer when Teri, Martha, and Sarah came in. They didn't see me. I watched as they ordered pizza and Cokes. It was neat they were there. I felt like a spy or something. But I was lonely. It'd be nice to talk to them instead of looking at them. Only there was that stuff about Martha seeing me drunk. Maybe if I sobered up somehow? No way. Besides, I didn't want to. I wanted to drink and socialize. That's why I came in the first place. That's what everybody did when they drank. It wasn't fair I had to hide in my room drinking by myself because my friends were so weird. No wonder everybody thought I was an alcoholic! If people acted normally about my drinking, I'd drink O.K. I started to get up, but then I sat down again. I remembered my promise to Martha, and the whole openness of the conversation. She trusted me, and I *had* promised. What I should do was sneak out the back entrance.

Why? another part of me shouted. I hide in my room to drink, and now I'm out at a restaurant and I run out the back door. I'm lonely and bored, and right over there are my closest friends. Not only that, but how come they didn't invite me in the first place? They probably thought I'd get smashed and embarrass them. They're the ones messing me over, if they only knew it. Teri dragging me to A.A., and Martha making rules, and Sarah acting funny over my drinking one lousy beer. I looked around at the other tables. Everybody was drinking and having a good time! Why should I drink Cokes just because my friends are such tight-asses? Stupid. I got up and made my way to their table, but I got a little scared on the way, so I decided I'd say hello and leave. Simple and acceptable.

Teri saw me coming and grinned until I lurched against a table. She started to get out of her chair to intercept me. I speeded up. Since I'd made my decision to say hello, I wasn't going to be stopped. "Hey, Teri, Martha, Sarah!" Sarah was the only one who greeted me half naturally. I sat down because I was weaving around too much standing up.

"What's happening?" I asked. I was trying to play it very cool, friend stops by to pay small visit at neighboring table.

"Not much," Sarah said. "We got bored, so we thought we'd go have a pizza. What'd you think of the decision?"

"Softball? It didn't bother me that much, not sure why, but—" The whole time we were talking, Martha had been sitting turned to one side, her face set. "Hey, Martha," I said finally, "what's the matter with you?"

She looked at me angrily. "I told you I didn't want to see you when you were drunk."

I shrugged. "I stopped by to say hello. I was here and all."

"O.K. You've said hello. Now split."

"God, Martha, you sure are in a nice mood."

"I was in a fine mood until you came falling by."

I looked at the table, hurt. "Gee, you don't have to treat me like that. We're supposed to be best friends."

"We are best friends, Niki, when you're sober. Now I want you to take off. You promised me."

"How come you didn't ask me to come in the first place?" I stalled.

"Because we decided to do it about nine-thirty. Spontaneous. We didn't have time to give you the required six-hour warning so you could lay off cocktails and dinner wine and after-dinner wine and before-bed beer. I knew you'd be smashed off your ass at nine-thirty, and I didn't want to see you drunk. That's why you didn't get invited." She turned away from me. "Since she doesn't seem to want to leave, I'm going to. I'll get a bus."

"No, no," Teri said. "We'll all leave." They started getting up.

"Wait! You haven't even gotten your pizza, Martha!" I grabbed her by the arm and yanked her back in the chair. "Be reasonable. I'll leave."

"Take your hand off my arm."

"All right, all right." I held up both hands. "See? Harmless." Teri and Sarah sat back down. "I want to say one thing first, and then I swear I'll leave. O.K.?"

"Niki," Martha warned.

"You make such a big deal out of everything, Martha. I was sitting over there thinking that the reason I drink so much is you and Teri bug me about it all the time. It's a self-fulfilling prophecy."

It took me three tries to get that out, but Martha sat and listened patiently. Then she said, "That is the stupidest thing I've ever heard you say. But I listened. Now get out."

"Why are you being—"

"Come on," Martha said furiously. They all got up again and walked out.

I trailed after them. "Look at all the other people in there drinking. Why are you such a goddamn prig?"

"I don't care about all those people!" Martha shouted, now that we were outside. "I care about you! And I can't stand to see you drunk! It's a very simple concept. I don't know why you can't understand it!"

"Hey—" Teri started.

"Anyway, Niki, I'm furious at you for promising first of all and breaking that promise, and then saying you'd leave and—"

177

"Martha?" Teri said.

I broke in sarcastically. "Teri's trying to give you some hot Al-Anon advice on how to deal with the drunk alcoholic. How are you ever going to learn if you won't listen?"

"Damn you, Niki, I don't care anymore what I say to you, you make me so angry. You think everything is some big joke."

"Aw, screw off, Martha!" We glared at each other, and I suddenly swung at her, a big roundhouse punch that missed by a mile.

Teri grabbed me and pinned my arms behind my back. I struggled, but I was much too weak and drunk to fight off Teri. "All right," Teri said calmly. "Let's cool it. Sarah, you and Martha follow me to Niki's house in my car. I'm driving her home."

"I can drive," I muttered. Only by this time Teri was more holding me up than holding me back.

Sarah reached over to Teri's pocket and took out her keys. "O.K.," she said. "We'll meet you there." The two of them went off down the street, Martha holding her back all stiff like a singed cat.

"O.K., hot shot," Teri said. "Where's your car?"

"You can let go now," I said weakly.

Teri let loose and I staggered back against the wall. "Teri? Why does Martha act like that?"

"Let's talk about it on the way. Where's the car?"

I thought. The car. Where did I put the car? "Oh, yeah," I said. "It's up there."

"O.K." We started walking. This time I held on to her. I was having a lot of trouble staying on my feet. Finally she put her arm around my waist. "You are really bombed," she said.

"Teri, why is Martha—"

"Here, give me your keys." I handed them to her and stumbled into the door. "Lemme help," Teri said.

Once we were in the car and under way, I tried again. "What is it with Martha? How come she's so hostile?"

Teri kneaded her fingers around the steering wheel. "She figures she can't do anything about your drinking, which is true. But that doesn't mean she has to watch it."

"But why is she hostile? She acted like I was a total piece of trash."

"Because it upsets her. I know that I have no responsibility over your drinking, so I can be with you without getting mad. Your being drunk doesn't mean I have to do anything. But Martha, see, she understands that intellectually, but she's not sure emotionally. She feels she's being a bad friend or something. She gets ticked off because you make her guilty. Plus," Teri said, looking at me, "you're a total idiot when you're drunk, and boring besides. So you're not exactly a desirable companion."

"Guess so," I mumbled. By this time, we were at my house, and I could see Sarah and Martha sitting in Teri's car with the motor running.

"Now listen," Teri said. "I don't want any more hassles. Forget Martha tonight. You'll make things worse if you try to talk to her again."

"I'll go right in the house."

Teri shut off the car and handed me the keys. "Cheer up," she said. "There's always a light at the end of the tunnel."

That sounded a little patronizing, but I decided to ignore it so I could concentrate on getting in the house. I congratulated myself when I did it without even looking at their car. I went to the refrigerator and got another beer. See, I forgot all about it, I told myself. Only I crept into the living room and peeked between the drapes. They were still there, talking, motor running. Wasting gas, I said to myself. I took a long pull on the beer, and loneliness hit me again like a steel glove—whap in the face. Why couldn't I be out there with them? If I was an alcoholic, I couldn't help it, right? They didn't have to be so mean. I looked at the beer in my hand. Then I heard them pull off.

I rambled around the house trying to amuse myself without waking up my parents. Reading didn't work, because I couldn't focus. And TV was too dumb. Everything was so boring! I couldn't stand it! Martha being such a drag had put me in a lousy mood. I'd been fine earlier, sitting at the restaurant watching people. If they hadn't come, I might have met somebody who didn't mind I was drunk. It was always possible. I staggered into the kitchen after another beer.

I woke with a start, as if somebody had jabbed me with a pin. The first thing I became aware of was a funny noise near my head. What the— It was the phone off the hook, making that stupid beeping noise. What's it doing off the hook? And what's it doing in my room? I looked at it. I must have called somebody last night. The pizza parlor flitted around at the edges of my memory, but I didn't want to let it in, I didn't want to— Martha! Oh, God, I must have called Martha! I went out to the kitchen quickly, trying to distract myself with motion. It didn't work. I remembered swinging at her, and her face flushed with anger. She must hate me. She must totally despise me. I had to know. I ran back to my room and dialed her number with shaky fingers. Martha, don't be mad, don't hate me. I couldn't help it.

Her father's sleepy voice came on the line. I hadn't looked at the time, but surely— "This is Niki. Is Martha up yet?" There, that sounded normal.

Her father exploded. "Niki, do you realize it's seven o'clock in the morning? What the hell's the matter with you? What's so important you have to call at seven after calling last—"

The upstairs phone clicked in, and I heard Martha. "Daddy, let me talk to her."

180

"Now look, Martha," he said dubiously.

"Daddy!"

"Oh, all right!" He slammed down the phone. Jesus, I thought. Everything I do gets worse and worse.

"Aren't you going to say anything?" Martha said after a minute.

"I guess I called you last night?"

"You called all right. At midnight, at twelve-fifteen, at one, and at one-thirty. It was a lot of fun trying to get to the phone before my parents so they wouldn't hear all your obscenities in this slurred voice." She did a little imitation, and I groaned. "And now you're very sorry, right? It was so important to tell me how sorry you are that you had to wake me up after I'd finally gotten to sleep."

I couldn't say anything. I sat there holding the phone.

"What did you call about?" Martha shouted. "You must have had something to say."

I took a deep breath. "You're right, I called to apologize. I couldn't stand— I wanted to make things right again. I couldn't stand not knowing if you hated me. I forgot to look at a clock."

"You forgot. That's a good excuse. It's you first, all the time. Your freakouts are more important than anything else, even when you're supposedly apologizing. If you're upset, sure, call at seven in the morning. Screw Martha. You want to check to see if I'm still hanging on. Best friend Martha. I'm sick and tired of being messed over by you, Niki. You broke your promise, and I can't take it anymore! I can't take it!" She started sobbing. The sound pierced me like a knife.

"Martha, please, listen to me for a—"

Her voice hardened suddenly, and I shivered. "Niki, I've had it. I'm finished listening to you. You blame me, and you keep on making me crazy. I'm through! I don't want to see you or hear from you. I don't want you to call me, and if we see each other on the street, forget you know me."

"Martha! Martha! Don't say that! Martha!" I could hardly get her name out of my mouth I was crying so hard.

"I just said it," she answered wonderingly. The phone clicked in my ear.

"Oh, God, oh, God!" I rocked back and forth moaning, and my father rushed in, wearing his pajamas.

"Niki! What's the matter, honey? What happened?"

"Leave me alone!" I screamed at him. "Don't touch me!" I could feel myself getting hysterical and I had to get out. I pushed past him and slammed out the front door, barefoot but still dressed from last night. I ran crying in the early morning cool, oblivious to anything around me. I ran for what seemed like hours.

When I crept back, the house was empty. There was a note from my mother. "How can you treat your father like that?" it read. "He's terribly upset. I want you to apologize. I'll be home at three-thirty. Don't eat any ham. There's barely enough for dinner. Love, Joyce."

I stared at it, a meaningless jumble of words, and then fresh sobbing convulsed me. I grabbed my stomach and fell to my knees on the kitchen floor, mumbling, "Martha, Martha," over and over.

Somewhere a phone was ringing. I came out of my trance and ran to the table. I snatched up the receiver. "Martha?"

"No, it's me, Teri. Sorry to disappoint you like that. But I've got a message from her."

A message? I thought frantically. She won't see me, she has to send messages. Oh, God! Then I realized Teri was talking and I wasn't listening. "Teri, I'm sorry. What did she say?"

"She's sorry she was so cold on the phone," Teri repeated patiently. "She was angry, and she isn't now. She says for you not to hate yourself, that it was her decision, and she doesn't mean to lay anything on you. She thinks you have to go through this drinking thing, but she can't take it. She said for me to tell you she loves you."

"Why won't she tell me herself then?" My voice rose to a wail, and I started crying again. "I can't stand it, Teri! Why do I do these things?"

"Niki," Teri said.

"I don't know what to do, it goes on and on, there's no relief. How can she say not to hate myself? What does she expect?"

"Hey, Niki? How 'bout if I call Mandy and—"

I didn't listen. I was too embarrassed, sobbing and screaming on the phone this way to Teri. "Teri, I'm sorry. Oh, forget it!" I slammed down the phone and stared at it. Green, I thought. A green phone. You're losing your mind, part of me said. Another part started denying it, but mostly I was in shock, stripped of everything, a walking corpse that felt only pain. The only reason I could think of to go on living was as some kind of punishment for being so horrible. I didn't deserve the relief suicide would bring.

But then I thought, What if Teri calls Martha and tells her how upset I am? Martha said she still loves me. She might call. If only she'd call, then I'd be all right. I walked back and forth looking at the phone. Ring, ring, ring! Only it wouldn't. I got a magazine and spent an hour looking at disconnected words, glancing up at the phone the whole time. Another hour crept by. Finally I knew she wasn't going to call, that she'd left me all alone with myself.

Chapter XX

My parents couldn't miss my depression. I stumbled around the house in a gray funk so intense I walked into chairs and doors sober. After three days of questioning, my mother hit the jackpot. "Why hasn't Martha called? Did you two have an argument?"

"We didn't have an argument," I said wearily. "The Hauptmanns went away to their cabin for a month. I told you a long time ago they were going away in August." I had rehearsed this story the day before.

"I don't remember that. I didn't even know they had a cabin."

Martha's and my parents had only met a couple of times. Everything they knew about each other was funneled through us. Martha and I had used this conduit of misinformation several times in the past; now it was coming in handy again.

"They share it with three other families," I told Joyce. "They were scheduled for August this year, so Mr. Hauptmann arranged to take a long vacation."

My mother wasn't certain she believed me. No one likes to see her brilliant ideas torpedoed by what seems to be a logical explanation. She did put enough stock in my answer to begin looking for another solution.

To keep away from them, I stayed in my room. I couldn't go on hating myself forever, but it seemed that way for a while. I thought about running away and starting over. I made lists for trips I wouldn't take. I had fantasies of working on salmon boats in Alaska, where I didn't drink, where I had lots of friends. But every time the phone would ring, I was right back at home, waiting for Martha to miss me, Martha to forgive me. It was never her. Mandy called, but I was rude to her, and she gave up. I only wanted to talk to Martha, and Martha didn't want to talk to me.

Drinking in my room at night didn't kill the pain. When I was drunk, I was twice as lonely, especially since I had to drink on the sly for the most part. I went to a party with Sam once, but I ditched him and wandered around in a blackout for a few hours. I came to a half-mile from Martha's. It scared me. I wouldn't let myself leave my room after that if I'd had anything at all to drink. No cruising to the pizza parlor, no more parties. If I could have locked myself in a cage that opened automatically every morning, I would have done it.

One day I was so lonely I swallowed my pride and called Teri. Teri's mother answered. "Hi, Mrs. Cummings. Is Teri home?"

"No, sorry. She moved into an apartment yesterday with Martha Hauptmann. You want her number?"

"Sure," I mumbled. An apartment! With Martha! If I hadn't been drinking, if I'd stayed sober those times I stopped, I could have moved in with them too. I wrote down the number and stared at it. Should I call? Martha might answer; but if I asked for Teri, that would be all right, wouldn't it? I remembered Martha's face the night I swung at her. I crumpled the paper up in a ball and threw it away. At least I can go out at night now, I thought grimly. I don't even know where Martha lives. Instead of sitting around my room crying, I forced myself to drive up to the park to feed the ducks. As well as hiding my drinking from my parents, I was now trying to conceal my loneliness and depression. It was easier than answering a million well-intentioned questions.

I came home to a holocaust. My father was standing in the living room holding two empty fifths of rotgut gin from my bedroom. "Joyce cleaned your closet," he said.

Inappropriate as it seemed, I started laughing. I was sure some of the fury in his eyes was from the cheap labels. If I'd had Beefeaters or Bombay squirreled away, he might not have been so mad.

"Why are you laughing?" he shouted. I could hear my mother crying somewhere off toward the rear of the house.

His question sounded silly. I could be crying like my mother or screaming the way he was, but instead I was laughing. What did that prove?

"I don't know." I shrugged. I climbed up the stairs to my room and locked the door.

When I came back downstairs hours later, my father had a series of announcements. "You will not bring liquor in this house, you will not drink in this house, not beer, not—"

"Fine, fine," I muttered, avoiding his eyes. He slapped me so hard I flew across the room, my shoulders ending up against the fireplace.

"Carl!" Joyce shouted. "Carl, stop it!"

I laughed again. I couldn't help it. "Lucky it's not winter," I said, prying myself off the hearth. "I might have gotten burned." While I was trudging back to my room, I realized I didn't have to worry about going crazy anymore. I already was.

Next day there was a lock on the liquor cabinet, and the

bottles that had sat out on the kitchen counter were safely shut inside. The half-full fifth in my closet had disappeared along with the empties. The lock was just for show. Carl couldn't lock the wine cellar, not without going to an incredible amount of trouble, and there were still a couple of six-packs in the bar refrigerator. I ignored the lock, ignored their beer and wine. My mother had scrounged around in my wallet and taken my fake ID, but even that was O.K. The guy at the little grocery store hadn't asked for my ID in months. I began buying pints, the flat kind I could stick behind my radio with *Alcohol Dependence*. I laughed about that too.

I balanced on the knife edge of hysteria and depression for days. It was as if I was always hung over, forever caught in that world where nothing mattered, where the worst had already happened. I hardly thought about Martha anymore. I didn't think of anything. There was nothing anyone could do to me, and my parents seemed to sense it. They edged around the fringes of my life helplessly, afraid to peek inside.

The one reality I had to consider was money. I couldn't figure out why I wasn't getting any babysitting jobs. The Jacksons down the street still paid me twenty dollars a month to keep up their yard, but twenty dollars could stretch to only six of the cheapest pints. I stuck up signs at the laundromat and the supermarket. One afternoon I heard my mother say on the phone, "Niki? Oh, I'm sorry, she doesn't do babysitting anymore. She got a full-time job last week."

The idea of my mother lying woke me out of my lethargy. The pain I'd been jamming inside broke on me full-force, and I responded with anger. "What in the hell are you *doing?*" I hollered at her. "Are you nuts? I'm totally broke and you're turning down jobs?"

Joyce looked at me warily, as if she expected me to shatter into a million pieces, a human hand grenade that would destroy her too. She was frightened of me. I could see it in her eyes.

You've made your own mother afraid of you, I told myself. I couldn't stand it. I bolted to my room and wrestled my suitcase out of the closet.

"What are you doing?" Joyce shouted from the doorway.

I wouldn't look at her. I began ripping clothes off the hangers, stuffing things haphazardly in the suitcase. Her footsteps faded down the hall. Good. Then I heard frantic dialing. "Dr. Buehler? I'm sorry to bother you. Is Carl with you? To Mrs. Angles. Thank you." More dialing. I stopped to listen, and my energy ran out, drained by such an influx of self-hatred I could barely make it to the hall.

"Joyce!" I yelled. "Forget it! I'm not leaving." I closed the suitcase on all the jumbled clothes and stuck it back in the closet.

My father came home an hour or so later, and they talked for a while. They made some phone calls and talked again. Phoning some institution? Someone came to the door, and I tensed up. Nothing. More talk. Finally it began to get dark.

"Niki!" my mother called. "Tonight's our bridge night. We're leaving now. Goodbye."

" 'Bye!" my father echoed.

"See ya," I yelled, to let them know I was alive. What's the deal? For the past month they've been practically standing guard duty. I went out into the living room after the front door closed. A stack of Al-Anon literature sat on the coffee table. Oh, ho! That explained the phone calls and the visitor. Al-Anon was getting a good workout from Niki Etchen, star teenager.

I wandered into the kitchen, thinking vaguely about dinner. I rattled among cottage cheese containers until I gave up and snapped open a beer. Food was tasteless, and anyway it was

188

for people who wanted to live. Niki Etchen, the hot commodity. Hadn't I called myself that just a few months earlier? I could count up my successes on one hand. My great relationship with Chuck, my wonderful friendship with Martha, not to mention how I'd recovered that brave kid that stood on the Carmel cliffs. . . . I stared at the can of beer in my hand and felt such hopeless anger I crushed it in. Beer started flowing from the crack, and I threw it against the wall. Brilliant, I congratulated myself. I can get in a lot of pitching practice this way. Toss all the bottles and the cans and the glasses. Crayon strike zones on the walls of every room.

I went into the bathroom and got out a new package of razor blades. Then I hesitated, and I went back into the kitchen for a beer to give me courage. I gulped down a few slugs of wine from a bottle in the refrigerator and carried the beer into the bathroom. I tested the blade against my thumb. It was sharp. I sighted on my wrist and made a small cut, barely breaking the skin. A hairline of red popped to the surface. This would be easy, I told myself soothingly. You can do it. I put down the razor blade and drank more beer, trying not to think about what I had to do. I took up the razor blade again and traced a line along the cut I'd already made. It didn't hurt much. It was sort of interesting, like dissecting a frog in biology. I remembered my parents. They'd be sad to come home and find me. I started crying for them being so sad. They were fine now, I told myself. Al-Anon would explain it wasn't their fault. I smiled. Sure, they were fine. Actually, my being gone would be a big load off their minds.

Look, Niki, I commanded, Daddy always said don't be a quitter. Do it hard. This time it hurt, but I still wasn't getting anywhere. Blood was flowing into my cupped hand, but I hadn't hit an artery yet. Then I remembered the artery was under something, a ligament maybe? Something like that. I drank more beer, telling myself I had to do it superhard, just bear down, no screwing around. I finished the beer and went after another, wrapping a piece of toilet paper around my wrist. No point in leaving a mess. When I came back, the bleeding had almost stopped. I positioned the razor blade next to the cut and looked hard at my wrist. It was defenseless, sitting there waiting for me to cut it. I started feeling sorry for it. It hadn't done anything wrong. It wasn't fair to slash it all up, make it bleed. But then how could I kill myself? Maybe you don't want to, I thought. I tried to figure out what I did want. I wanted to stop hating myself, to stop feeling guilty all the time, to stop hurting people. I washed off my arm, poured the beer down the sink, and went to bed.

When I woke up, I decided to spend the whole day being nice to myself and not argue with myself once. I read a little, drew a picture, and finally, toward evening, I drove up to a hill overlooking the Golden Gate Bridge and watched the sunset. I felt calmer. If I liked my wrist enough not to cut it anymore, maybe I could learn to like the rest of me. It seemed sort of stupid, but it was worth trying. I had to get out of this hole I'd dug for myself. I could try being comfortable.

I didn't drink that night, or the next, or the next. I wasn't sure why I wasn't drinking, since I'd told myself I could do whatever I wanted, which included drinking. When I thought about it, I'd say, Yeah, but then you couldn't read that book, or, you could, but you know you'd be twice as lonely. So I didn't drink. My parents weren't hovering over me constantly, and that made it easier. I didn't have to conjure up explanations for them. All that could come later. I had to concentrate now on myself. Those A.A. slogans—First things first and One day at a time—started to make sense.

I began going to the library on campus at night. I felt much better there than at home. I read novels and magazines and watched people come in and out of the building, figuring out life histories for them. I thought occasionally about getting the books for my university classes, but somehow I didn't feel so frantic about that anymore. It'll work out, I told myself. Don't hassle it before it happens.

Midway into the third week of not drinking, I called Sarah and asked if she'd catch for me. "Sure," she said. "I need the exercise. We could throw each other grounders, and I could bat while you pitch."

When we got together, she didn't ask about my drinking, and I didn't volunteer any information. She accepted me as I was. We played around together a few afternoons a week. It was nice and easy, mellow.

Then school started. I felt as if I was being dragged screaming into a maelstrom of activity. Mitch wanted me to negotiate a new contract with the printers plus cover the football team practices. Sarah told me Scotty had decided the only way she would be allowed to keep the softball team going was as a concession, so she was fighting for a women's basketball team. Scotty's theory was they would refuse the basketball team, but they could hardly axe softball too. The halls were full of faceless bodies and screaming voices. I was lonely. Every time I walked around the buildings, I'd expect to run into Martha or Teri or Frank. Even Sam was gone. I'd forgotten he was a senior too. Jeff, the big kid, approached me about a lunch booze run on my ID, but I told him to forget it. After three days of school, I knew I couldn't stand it.

I went to see Mr. Mansfield. "Could I stop coming to high school? The only requirements I have left are civics and P.E., and I can fulfill those at the university."

The Manse peered at me over his glasses. "Yes, you *could*," he answered slowly. "But why don't you hang around? You'd be a shoo-in for valedictorian."

The expression on my face squelched that idea. "O.K.," he sighed. "I'll do the paperwork today. Come back in an hour or so."

I raced out of his office and dashed about saying goodbye to my teachers. Mitch was sad but philosophical. "I guess we can get along without you. We'd have to next year anyway. Good luck in college."

I walked around the grounds, working up enough nerve to go to the P.E. building. Scotty and I had barely spoken a word to each other since the scene at the hospital. I knocked at her office door.

"Come in." She was sitting there smoking her cigarette.

"You're going to die if you keep smoking those things," I said.

She shrugged and looked at me.

"I came to say goodbye. I'm leaving school."

"You're what?" she yelped. She started to rise from her chair.

"No, no, it's not like that. I'm already accepted to college, and I go on there now instead of staying."

"Oh," she said and sank back down again. "Niki, we've had a lot of trouble between us. I'm sorry—"

"Hey," I interrupted, raising my palm at her. "Don't start apologizing. If you did, then I'd have to, and it'd take me a few days to run through all the shit I've pulled."

She grinned. "That's true. Can't you ever talk without swearing?"

I thought about it. "Guess not," I said. "It's like your smoking. Goodbye."

She came around the desk and hugged me. I thought I might start crying. I pulled back. She smiled at me and clapped me on the shoulder. "Go on, kiddo. Come back and see some of our games."

192

"O.K.," I yelled. I was already out the door.

After a whole six weeks of not drinking had gone by, my biggest problem was still loneliness. University classes had started, and they were fine. I ended up taking a whole different schedule from the one I'd planned, and I longed to tell Martha, so she could laugh about it. I thought of calling her, to tell her I wasn't drinking, but I was afraid I'd drink right after. I wasn't making anybody any promises. I was still using my system of whatever I want, do it. It seemed to work. I didn't want to drink. The rest of the stuff I was doing felt too good. It was great being at the university, because I was a cipher, one student out of thousands. Nobody knew me, and there weren't any pressures to be the best this or the greatest that. One day I ran into Frankie on campus, and she tried to convince me to come to a meeting. I put her off, but it started me thinking. I could see Teri, I thought. And Mandy. She *had* been nice. And Teri could tell me about Martha.

Finally, one lonely night, I crept into a Fellowship. The A.A. meeting was mobbed, about forty people. I needed a couple of people to talk to, not a huge mob. Then I remembered Al-Anon met a half-hour later. I thought about it. That would be good. Smaller, less hassley, and I wouldn't have to say I was an alcoholic. I was down on labels. I was a person that wanted to stop drinking, that's all. I got a cup of coffee and went into the Al-Anon room off the back, juggling my books and the cup, trying not to spill the coffee. When I looked up, Martha was staring at me across the table. She had books laid out all over.

"Oh!" I said stupidly. We continued looking at each other, and finally I mumbled, "Sorry," and started to back out.

She jumped up from the table. "Niki! Wait! Don't leave. I was so surprised I couldn't think of anything to say. Don't act like that."

"Huh? Like what?" I was embarrassed. I felt two inches high, a disgusting idiot. I hated myself all over again, remembering what I'd done to her.

"You look ashamed, or apologetic, or— Oh, God, I'm so stupid! I've been going to—"

"Wait," I interrupted. "How come you're here anyway? I thought you'd given up on me." I was standing stiffly, holding my books in front of me. I was afraid of her, afraid of how much she meant to me. I didn't want to be hurt.

She sat down and looked at me standing over her. "I had. I have. At first I kept going because I wanted support for not seeing you. I knew you were waiting for me to call, going through hell, hating yourself. But I couldn't stand feeling so responsible, as if I was an absolute failure all the time because I couldn't get you to see you had to stop drinking. Then I talked to Teri and Mandy and Frankie. I realized I wasn't responsible, that I could set limits, like only seeing you when you were sober and not feel guilty myself when it got messed up. I could make a decision myself, whether to see you or not, day by day, not insist on a bunch of rules—so I've been coming to try to get that together, only I— I was afraid I couldn't do it, afraid I'd hurt you again. I don't know," she finished.

"I haven't drunk for six weeks," I said. I was still stiff. Why couldn't I unbend?

"Six weeks? That's fantastic! Unbelie—"

"But I'm not making anybody any promises," I broke in. "This is for me, as long as I want it. That's all."

"Promises?" she echoed. "But that's why I didn't call you. I was afraid to promise you I could handle your drinking when I didn't know if I could. . . . Hey, remember when I said we worried about each other too much? That we had to have confidence? Maybe we could not have expectations."

"Make a promise not to have promises?" I said, shifting my books around. They were suddenly heavy.

"Oh, God, Niki," she moaned, suddenly bursting into tears. "Stop looking at me as if you're frightened to death. I can't stand it! I'm sorry!"

I blinked at her, amazed, and then I threw my books on the table and put my arms around her. "Martha! Martha! Don't say you're sorry! I'm the one that should be apologizing. Jesus, I totally screwed you over."

"You didn't!" Martha cried. "It was me trying to be so damned helpful. I set myself up for everything that happened."

"That's not true. I was selfish. Listen, Martha, you were right. Everything you said that morning when I called, about only being concerned about my own freakouts, and calling to see if you were still there, and— Hell, you couldn't help feeling guilty either. It's no fun to see your best friend crawling around on the sidewalk drooling in a drunken stupor— Martha? Don't cry."

"I'm not crying anymore," she said, her voice muffled by my jacket. "I'm laughing. This is so silly. We're both afraid of calling each other because we think the other one is going to have expectations, and now we're arguing over who was more at fault. It's ridiculous!"

"That's true," I said, laughing too. "Hey, Martha? Let's pledge not to make promises. O.K.?"

"O.K., Niki. And no being down on ourselves either."

"Martha!" I said severely. "You're doing it again! If we want to wallow in self-pity or depression, we'll wallow."

"You're right. Hey, Niki? I missed you a whole lot."

"I missed you too."

Then the door opened, people came in and the meeting started. Martha and I sat through it smiling at each other, both of us happy as hell to be there.

Linnea Due was born in Berkeley, California. She graduated from Sarah Lawrence College and holds a graduate degree in Criminology from the University of California at Berkeley. Although she now divides her time between writing and working at a newspaper in Berkeley, she played on an Oakland league softball team for many years. She is also the author of *Give Me Time* and is at work on a new novel.

▣spinsters | *aunt lute* ▣

Spinsters/Aunt Lute Book Company was founded in 1986 through the merger of two successful feminist publishing businesses, Aunt Lute Book Company, formerly of Iowa City (founded 1982) and Spinsters Ink of San Francisco (founded 1978). A consolidation in the best sense of the word, this merger has strengthened our ability to produce vital books for diverse women's communities in the years to come.

Our commitment is to publishing works that are beyond the scope of mainstream commercial publishers: books that don't just name crucial issues in women's lives, but go on to encourage change and growth, to make all of our lives more possible.

Though Spinsters/Aunt Lute is a growing, energetic company, there is little margin in publishing to meet overhead and production expenses. We survive only through the generosity of our readers. So, we want to thank those of you who have further supported Spinsters/Aunt Lute—with donations, with subscriber monies, or with low and high interest loans. It is that additional economic support that helps us bring out exciting new books.

Please write to us for information about our unique investment and contribution opportunities.

If you would like further information about the books, notecards and journals we produce, write for a free catalogue.

Spinsters/Aunt Lute
P.O. Box 410687
San Francisco, CA 94141